STONE OF DESTINY

Juniper Samoni Trilogy

NADINE TRAVERS

Fiction
Publication

CONTENTS

License Note

For more information:
http://www.nadinetravers.com
https://www.supernaturalintelligenceagency.com

Dépôt legal

Bibliothèque & Archives nationales du Québec 2021

Bibliothèque & Archives du Canada 2021

❀ Created with Vellum

BLURB

Stone of Destiny calls out to her to save it. The clock is ticking, and evil is not too far behind.

Juniper's coven has assigned her a dangerous mission: to brave the magic cave in Scotland and save the Stone of Destiny. If the stone falls in to the wrong hands, the wielder can use the power to make everyone their slaves.

Now the fate of the paranormal community is put to Juniper... but if evil lurking in the shadows beats her to the treasure, there will be no turning back.

Fans of Ilona Andrews and the Uncanny Kingdom will devour Stone of Destiny, book one in the Juniper Samoni Trilogy.

Buy this action-pack, suspenseful urban fantasy supernatural thriller now.

CHAPTER ONE

JUNIPER

In the gathering place again, I take a breath. The air carries the scent fresh almost cold of witch magic. The ceiling and walls are made of wood, centuries old. Still healing from my last mission, I've been summoned by the Elders, the sages of the witching world.

"Child, enter the circle of truth," a voice commands.

I didn't see them come in, so I jump a little. Five Elders take their seats in the circle that's been drawn on the ground.

I approach the gold circle, the edges etched in a pattern I don't recognize. "Elders, you summoned me."

"You have news, Juniper. Disturbing news. You must tell us everything."

I take another deep breath and enter the circle. It alights as I step in, turning brighter, twisting and wiggling as though made alive.

I study the five Elders. Their age as well as their power are mysteries that would frighten some members of my faction, but I know Elders want the best for us all. I close my eyes, letting the light and the energy of the circle of truth fill me. I surrender myself to it.

I WAS IN A JUNGLE CORRIDOR. The luscious green walls of a maze in the Amazon rainforest stood tall all around me. I answered the call to rescue the Toadstone. Someone wanted to take its power for themselves.

Along with the Supernatural Intelligence Agency, we were investigating an organized team of powerful individuals that we suspected of working against our community.

"Give the stone to us!"

I turned around and considered the three of them: a demon, a vampire, and a werewolf. Each one was a member of a species that shouldn't be partnering with the other two.

I raised my sword in one hand and my gun in the other, and I commanded the stone to sink into my skin for safe keeping. Then I turned to my three opponents. "I'll never let you have it. Give up now."

They would fight for the stone.

I darted away, and I didn't look back. Someone hit me, and I fell to the ground. I rolled to the side and jumped back to my feet.

The vampire appeared in front of me. He would be faster and stronger, but the demon was the strongest of the three.

I conjured an ultraviolet blade. Blue luminescence burst forth on my katana.

The vampire charged, but I moved to the side and sliced his chest with my magic sword.

"Argg!" the vampire screamed. "You bitch!" He charged again. He'd either never faced a Witch Warrior in combat, or he was a fool. There was, of course, the third option – he could be a pureblood, born a vampire. In that case, my sword could only slow him down.

Witch Warriors are trained to be the best. We never know what we will encounter on our missions, so the coven trains us in all warrior skills, whether hand to hand combat or weaponry. We also learn the strengths and weaknesses of all the species.

The werewolf joined the vampire. "I'm going back. Leave me with the stone," the beast cried.

Great. Now I had to fight two at the same time.

I grabbed my gun and cast a spell. "Argentum indicibus excitant!"

A silver light enveloped my gun, and I fired. I missed the werewolf by an inch. "That's a warning, dog. Stop, or the bullet goes to your head next time."

He bared his teeth.

As I thought.

He charged again, but the demon bore down on us.

Fuck. *My teleport circle wasn't close enough.*

I needed one less enemy to fight. The vampire healed slowly, the magic of my sword made sure of it. So I took aim at the werewolf.

"Give it back to us." The deep growl of the demon filled my ear. I gagged as a disgusting stench filled the air. Why on earth did the demon smell like that? How could the werewolf, with his enhanced sense of smell, tolerate it?

I squeezed the trigger. My bullet hit the target.

The werewolf yelped and fell on the ground. The vampire stood beside the demon, and they glanced at each other.

I tried to back toward my circle in the forest. The vampire lunged at me. I fired several more shots, but missed all of them.

He reached for something hidden behind his back. "You must die. Meet my witch killer. You'll enjoy its effect on you."

Oh. Fuck. Not that. I'd heard about witch killers, those feisty, murderous little dark faeries, but I've never had to fight one. Between the witch killer and the demon, I was about to be in deep shit. I never knew that a dark faerie would pledge herself to a vampire. I tried to remember my species studies and training.

Fuck. That didn't help.

"That stone doesn't belong to you," I yelled. Then I fled into the forest. I had to reach my magic circle and get the Toadstone to the

coven. That was my number one priority. If other paranormal species were cooperating to achieve a goal, something bigger was going on, some larger plan.

The middle of the Amazon rainforest wasn't the best place to investigate the mystery. Witch Warriors traveled around the world, wherever our missions took us. It wasn't the first time different members of species and factions worked together toward the same goal. But, with the Supernatural Intelligence Agency, we were investigating the newest occurrence, digging to find the answer.

I was almost in the travel circle. A few more steps would get me out of this place.

"Don't go further! Give us the stone." The vampire yelled from nearby. How come the vampire could stand the sunlight?

A chant filled the air. No.

A witch! She was casting a protective spell on the vampire. Why would she work with them?

"No, you're not going to have it!" My lungs burned from all the running and casting, but I pressed forward. Ahead, my transport circle waited. As long as I breathed, the circle would remain. I'd already beaten the werewolf, and the injured vampire fought more slowly with the wound from my katana.

More opponents approached. The dark faeries caught up with me. The leader sneered.

"You think you can get rid of me?" the witch screamed. She summoned her magic.

I ran faster. That circle was the only way out. The situation was getting out of hand as more reinforcement arrived. Outnumbered and exhausted, I fought, pushing myself even as my energy drained away.

The demon advanced. Alone, my katana couldn't pierce the demon's thick skin, but with the help of a lava enhancement spell, I sliced through his arm.

He screamed, grabbing his wrist.

I still needed to beat the witch. She protected that vampire. If I could halt her spell-casting, I'd be able to end the vampire.

I dodged him, but the witch remained. I rushed at her with my sword held forward. One shifter grabbed my weapon, but he let me go when I kicked him in the balls. The witch blinked at me and then teleported out of my reach, stopping her incantation.

I peppered two of the four attacking shifters with magic bullets and started casting a spell to bind the witch's mouth, but one of the two remaining werewolves hit me and interrupted my casting.

I bolted away. I had to neutralize that witch. My sword flamed in a magic power of its own as it cut into her arm, but the witch's magic protected her, and my vicious slash that should've severed a limb left only a scratch.

A werewolf's shove slammed me into the ground. He landed on top of me, his saliva dripping on my face. Another werewolf tried to capture my weapon, but I held onto it. They had a protection spell that prevented me from touching them. I kicked like a madwoman and eventually managed to scramble away.

From my left, a figure —big and fast —barreled toward us and came to a stop beside me.

"Need help?" the newcomer asked.

I pointed my gun and thrust my katana toward him.

"Hey, hey. I'm not with them. I've been watching, and I think you're outnumbered," he teased.

I wasn't in the mood for joking. "What the fuck are you teasing me about?" He was some kind of shifter, with a very old aura. "Now is not the time," I added.

The werewolves came at us, then, but my new friend avoided them easily.

"Bad dog," he told one of them as he punched him right on the nose, shattering the snout.

I stared. I had to join in the fight, but I gaped instead. How was he able to crush, not just break, a werewolf's nose like that?

The werewolf yipped in pain, and the others backed away, making space between them and the new threat.

I was tempted to let him deal with the rest. He seemed strong enough to neutralize them, and I still had a mission. But I was so out of focus, and one of the other werewolves attacked me with the help of the dark fae.

That bitch.

The attacker reached for the stone embedded in my skin. I conjured a spell and re-secured the stone. A magic bullet waited in the gun I held with my other hand.

I sneered at the two. Fighting it out was my only option.

"You will not have it," I screamed at them.

My new friend, for now, ran toward me. He had his fun with the other werewolves, but this one was big and enhanced by that dark fae.

I was drained, my casting getting weaker. I hadn't slept at all for two days.

I glanced at the shifter, the man from nowhere. "Need help," I said.

"What's that?" he asked.

I didn't like the situation at all, and I didn't like asking, but now he teased me with it.

He smiled at me, but the demon appeared behind him. The demon punched him, and the man took the full blast. He spun around to face the demon.

If he was happy moments earlier, he wasn't then. He cracked his neck. "You're a fucker. You know that, demon? I will teach you some manners."

He launched himself at the demon, fists flying, jabbing and punching.

What kind of shifter was he?

My circle was close, but two werewolves blocked my path. I ran toward them, shooting with my gun, but they dodged each projectile. One advanced on me, his claws and fangs out. I attacked him with my katana, and he yelped with each cut.

My chest heaved, not only from the run and fight, but from my magic stamina being almost gone. I studied the mysterious shifter. He was gorgeous by all means: his body stretched, his muscles rippling in

"What did the message say?" Jeremy asks.

I scowl at him. For sure, vampires don't feel the cold either.

"A small team is going to join us, and bring something to help us in our search for the hidden magic door." A smile spreads on my face.

"What it is, love?" Sophia asks as I study the horizon behind us, trying to make out the approaching figures in the pouring rain.

I point, and she looks.

"Reinforcements, I believe," Jeremy tells her. His eyesight is better than hers. Better than mine, too, since I can sooner smell them than see them.

I howl at the new arrivals. "Lucas!" I launch myself at my beta and draw him into a crushing hug.

"Alpha, we are here to help you," Lucas offers.

I clap him on the back and scan the group that came with him. "You brought Joseph, Brad and Carl, but who are the others?"

"We've got a demon – lower class, says he wants things to change. He is not a half-breed, but probably has some human blood, since he could do things by himself without the group." He waved to the woman. "And this is Clara. She's an earth witch."

"Happy to be reunited with my pack and to meet the rest of you. We have a mission to do. Are you all briefed?"

Clare, the earth witch, steps forward. "The Lady instructed us to give you this," she says, handing me a large ring. I turn it over in my hand, sensing its power through its magical energy.

"Apparently," she says, "that stone we're looking for is part of the history of Robert the Bruce. We believe that he used the stone to raise the rebellion against the English. "

"Do I have to wear it?" I ask Lucas.

"The Lady said that the ring will tell us if it needs to be used. A part of its magic role is to influence us to go toward the stone, but also to influence others to help us," Lucas says.

My wolf growls, deciding the matter — I won't wear it. "Love, can you cast something so that we can't lose it? My wolf is against the idea of me wearing it."

Sophia smiles at me and kisses me. "Sure, my love." She takes it and places it on my right pectoral muscle. As soon as she starts her incantation, my skin grows around the ring to hide it, like a sealed pocket.

After Sophia finishes, Clara gives me a letter from the Lady containing coordinates to find the hidden cave entrance on the biggest isle. I suspected it'd be there, but with magic you never know what is hidden.

"Does the note say anything about hidden traps?" asks Jeremy. "We can probably expect those, considering the cave is magically protected."

"No, the only warning is to watch out and not believe what we see. Now, it's time we move. Who's joining us?" I look at Lucas. "Other members of our pack."

That's better. I see that my pack is starting to think outside of werewolves for their mates. That will bring strength to our pack, but also means they'll be willing to fight for our cause and their future children's.

"Ok, let's go. The sooner we're done, the sooner we'll be able to celebrate," I say, hoping to fire them up for this fight.

"Whatever they throw at us, Alpha, we'll fight it. For the freedom of our factions, and to bring more fated mates to us and strengthen the pack."

I smile and put my hand on his shoulder. "I could not have said it better."

As we're leaving, Lucas texts the coordinates to the other team and nods at me.

Now, I hope that we've arrived first and that we'll avoid

traps along the way, even though my gut tells me otherwise. We just have to be prepared for anything.

I close my eyes and picture my wolf. We are on the same page, both wanting to make the faction divisions fall in order for all of us to be free to love whomever we want.

It's time to shake things up in the paranormal community.

~

JUNIPER

Okay. I know this is stupid. I should have watched where I was going.

But that pull, that sense of the stone, distracts me from those huge traps. I squat as arrows fly overhead. Lucky that Lilandra isn't here — she would lecture me on all my mistakes. There has to be a device or a lever around here that stops the mechanism, although now that the sequence has started, disarming it will be tricky.

I sprint across the floor. Another mechanism clicks below me. I cast a speed spell to make my legs pump harder and faster to outrun whatever's coming.

The traps will only impact the space they're created to guard. If I can get out of the way, I will be able to catch my breath. I really hope that I'm running the correct direction. I'm aiming toward the pull, and the sensation is getting stronger. It's the only way I know that I'm on the right path.

It's so dark inside the cave. My running spell takes focus away from maintaining my magic lights, and the light dims enough for me not to see my path anymore. I trip on the uneven terrain and hit the ground hard.

I shake my head and barely make out the spikes jutting up out of the floor in time to dodge them. A loud crash makes the ground vibrate. That's never a good sign. I climb to my feet, but my ankle hurts enough to slows me down. The exit is still so far away.

Someone slams into my back and picks me up, carrying me along faster, until my feet lift off the ground.

I turn this way and that, trying to figure out what's going on. I know it's a male by his smell, but the scent triggers something inside me and I recognize him in a heartbeat, my fists suddenly itching to punch him. It's the man who saved me in the Amazon a couple of days ago. That interfering son of a...!

He carries me through the exit as another loud noise sends the caves shaking. Everything is a trap now. We'll both be dead in a matter of seconds.

He breathes heavily in my ear. "That was close."

I conjure a healing spell for my ankle. It's just a slight sprain, but enough to be annoying. "You again." I don't know why, but he makes me lose my shit.

"You're welcome. Don't mention it," he answers, setting me down.

The bastard. "I didn't thank you."

"But I'm sure you wanted to."

I take a deep breath, seeking self-control. I've got to have some of it left somewhere. I shove him. He's way too close to me.

He lets me go but stays close. "You need to be more careful or you'll get yourself killed. This place is ancient and full of traps. "

For a woman, I'm tall, but he is so much taller than I am. The way he towers over me makes me feel small, and I really don't like it.

"I'm careful," I say. "It's not my first mission, and it will not be my last, either." I back up a little but he catches me.

"Careful, woman. This place is huge and magically protected."

I roll my eyes. "I'm aware. I'm used to this kind of situation. This is my *job*." I focus again on my light spell to illuminate the surroundings. I have no clue where this quest ends, but I need to get there and fast. The pull in my gut tells me that I'm not the only one here – enemies are inside the cave, too. I tip my head to the side. The stone wants me to save it.

"What are you doing here?" I ask.

He scowls at me. "Oh, where are my manners? I'm Drake. What's your name?"

"Juniper. I need to bring a stone relic to safety. It's calling me to help it." He needs to leave me alone – I don't have the time or the luxury of to explain anything further.

He looks me over. "You're a Witch Warrior?" he asks.

I nod, but add nothing else. The last thing I need is him following me around. I frown at him. Where had he come from?

I scrutinize him, really studying him this time. I have to admit that the man is gorgeous, but there's more to him than that. For starters, he's a kind of shifter I've never encountered before.

I squint at him. "What are you?"

He smiles. "You'll have to wait to find out. When you do, I will tell you a secret that will intrigue you, too."

He's a wacko. That's my best guess.

I march up to him and poke his chest. "Look, mister, I don't know what you are, but you better not turn out to be an enemy, because that will end very badly for you. I know you're not a ghost. So let me ask again: *what are you*?"

⚬

DRAKE

I love seeing her like this, all pissed off about what I just said.

I'm old, very old. I'm probably the last of my kind, or close enough to that.

It's been a while since I have had fun like this. My fated mate is something else. She's a Witch Warrior, but I suspect there's more to her. So young, so full of sass.

I must keep her intrigued if I want to win her.

I gesture toward her finger.

Her touch isn't sexual, but it brings me comfort. "What do you have to say?" She dares me.

I give her a half-smile. "Nothing. I have my secrets, just like you have yours. Until you tell me yours, mine will remain hidden."

She's screams at me, venting her frustration. At least that's my guess.

"You're lucky that I'm on a mission. Are you lost? How did you get in?" she asks.

It's almost a torture to be so close to her, yet unable to have my way with her, play with her, flirt and entice her. She will discover more with time, but for now, I don't want her to be so furious that she wants to flee. I need her close: the first step in our bonding is to kiss her and exchange energy. A passionate kiss will mingle our DNA and start a connection that will help her to fully understand what I am.

I lean against the wall. "I came through the same door you did. I'm not lost. I'm following you."

She comes very close, her jaw clenched, her face filled with emotions. "Impossible, unless you can sprout wings or a use flying spell. So which one is it?"

I don't respond to her question. I want her on edge.

"Whether you like or not, I'm following you. In time, you will learn to trust me."

She doesn't reply and shifts from side to side. I suspect her relic's call getting stronger, pulling at her body. I need to know more so I could help her, but under no circumstances can I afford to lose her. The consequences would be too horrible to imagine.

CHAPTER SEVEN

DONOVAN

WE ARRIVE AT ONE OF THE BIGGEST ISLANDS IN THE ISLE OF Skye. It's close to midnight, and the weather is terrible, but the conditions will help us remain unseen. I suppose this is normal weather for this place. It's nothing like Montreal.

I glance at my mate. She holds a warming spell around her. We werewolves don't need one, much like vampires. The weather doesn't affect either of us. I study the demon. The cold must not bother him either. The only concern is the earth witch who I suspect is Lucas' mate: he keeps her warm, and she puts the same spell around herself that most witches use, but hers seems less effective.

"Is this the place?" Sophia asks me.

I take her hand and kiss her knuckles. "Yes, it is, love." It's well hidden from humans – I wonder how many years, if not centuries, it has been hidden even from us, paranormal creatures. If I were a human, I never would've known that there is more than meets the eye on this island. "Do you feel the magic?"

Sophia nods. I go over the Lady's instructions. I have the ring that's linked to the Stone of Destiny embedded in my skin.

"There's some very old magic here. What are we supposed to do?" Sophia asks.

"According to the Lady, I should just stand in front of the magic entrance, and the ring should do the rest."

"I understand, love. I know by the energy fields that the entrance is there." She points to the far side of the island. "We need to go there."

I consider the team. For sure, witches won't have any problem getting there. The vampire won't either, but a were-wolf and a demon? That's another story. "How?"

"We need to use both of our magic. I need to be close to open it and so all of us will be inside." Sophia nods to Clara. "If she brings the earth high enough, I will be able to solidify it with my fire. That way we'll have a path to get there."

I kiss her. "Good idea. Work it out with her. We need to be on the other side."

She approaches the girl, and I let them figure out the details. It will take some time for them to create the path.

"Alpha?"

"Yes, Lucas."

He shifts to study the witch. "I know she's my mate." He looks back at me.

I smile. For a werewolf, finding your mate is a big thing. "I'm happy for you. I'm sure she will be suitable."

His shoulders droop. He must have been afraid to tell me.

"You didn't mark her yet?" I ask.

"No, I wanted to talk to you first."

"I'm mate to a witch, too, you know. I'm sure we will not be the only ones. I saw other pairings starting to form in the community. Those enforcing faction segregation will have no choice but to break the boundaries down. You don't go against a fated mate pairing. That's impossible. Not only for us, but for a lot of species."

He nods rapidly. "True. What other pairings have you seen?"

"I've learned that daywalkers can mate. Not only that, but they can bond with a werewolf. I saw not one, but two pairs like this. I also know that half-demons can pair with vampires. Beliefs are starting to change, making us find our mates differently. The faction system doesn't work anymore because it never evolved. Luckily, we have access to the neutral zone. Without it, we would never have been able to find each other, and most of the old species would have gone extinct."

Lucas doesn't answer. He's deep in thought. It's not a story anymore, but a fact. We need to let the faith decide for us, to make a better match. That the only way to make sure the bloodline is right.

"I have heard about occurrences like this, Alpha. I thought it was just gossip or stories that people make up, but you tell me you saw it yourself?"

I nod to Lucas. "Yes, that's why I do what I do. You didn't understand me in the beginning, but I couldn't tell you about Sophia without being challenged. You know how packs work."

"How many years have you been mate to Sophia?"

"Almost five now. I mark her, but not in our usual way. She's a witch, yes, but my wolf knows that she's the one. You know now, too. You are fated to be with a witch."

Lucas turns to study at Clara. He grins. "I met her in the neutral zone a year ago. I didn't understand what happened then, and I couldn't talk to anyone about it. It's still forbidden. The only one who knew was my twin sister. She understood. Later, I discovered that her mate is a vampire."

I gape at him shock. A vampire? An old enemy, in love with a werewolf.

"Yeah, I know. She's tried to break it off – a link that isn't breakable. Even she wanted me to let go of my connection to my fated mate, despite knowing that it will never be broken as long as we both live. You said that the faith wants to restore something. I believe it. I researched it, because if we continue the way it is, species will eventually give in to their instinct. Vampires need their fated mate to make a pureblood vampire. Our beasts know when we meet our mate, and will not accept anyone else. For centuries, some of us were lucky to find mates among humans, but I can see now that the times have changed, and I'm with you to the end."

I smile. I know I can trust him; he is my beta. I take a deep breath. "Now, it's time to enter that place and search for that stone."

Lucas smiles and nods. Our mates have worked things out, and we have a way to cross the water. I chuckle.

Sophia, love of my life... she will never stop impressing me.

∾

JUNIPER

The man seems amused. I tap my foot, waiting for him to turn around and leave, but he isn't getting the message.

"Whatever," I snap. "If you'll excuse me, I will resume my mission. As far as I'm concerned, you can get lost." I move away – I have my own problems to focus on. Why is he even here? He gets under my skin so easily, and I'm not sure why.

"I will follow you. You never know when I will save you again," he says.

I close my eyes and start to count backwards from ten. I

really need to calm myself. Where's that peace and focus Lilandra was always promising me when she taught me that? Apparently, the only thing she was right about is that my temper will get me into trouble.

"I don't care. I got something to do, and you can go to hell for all I care," I say, turning on my heel.

I march down the corridor, and he tags along. It's large enough for both of us to walk side by side. I feel the pull again as we come to an intersection in the tunnel. I test the emissions from the stone, trying to determine which direction is the one I need.

"And?" he asks.

I almost forgot about him. "Stay quiet. I have a job to do."

He crosses his arms on his chest. He seems amused again, but I'm not sure.

The pull is stronger on the left side. I move toward it.

"You think that's the spot?" he asks.

"I'm led by a gut feeling. It pulls me along. It's stronger towards the left. If you want to take the right path, be my guest."

He shakes his head. "I'm not leaving you.."

"You've got a lot of questions to answer, and until you do, I'm not talking to you."

He stands there in silence, just staring at me. He may be sexy, but he's a pain in my ass right now.

"You asked a lot of them," he says, "but I'm not ready to share the answers. You need to tolerate me like you said you would."

I'm losing patience. Lilandra would have said that you remain silent until you're able to confront the cause of your anger. I am not even going to look at him; I take a deep breath and focus on my mission instead. The first rule of being a Witch Warrior is that the relics are always the top priority. In any case, that's my main goal. No magical object should be allowed to fall into the wrong hands.

He follows me down the left path. "Silent treatment, really?"

"I warned you," I shrug. "I have a mission to do, and that's my priority."

He continues to walk beside me. I try to forget about him, every part of him. I push aside all the emotions he causes when he is close to me. Our mission is bringing the stone back. Even my life is expendable, but the relic is the priority.

I continue to walk down the left path. The tunnel narrows slightly, but Drake stays behind me. I thank the elements he chooses to be quiet. The pull on my magic gets stronger as the space we are in gets tighter.

"Are you sure that's the right direction?" he asks.

I take a deep breath. "Look. I didn't ask you to follow me. You can go back and do what you want. I don't care," I tell him, looking at him over my shoulder.

He doesn't answer, but his cocky grin is gone. He looks at the wall and then at me with a tumultuous expression, and I can't tell if he's fighting his inner beast or himself.

A hundred yards later, the corridor becomes so narrow that we have to turn sideways to walk.

He grabs my hand. "You're sure?"

I meet his gaze. I didn't notice his eye color before, but his mesmerizing irises change from light green to very bright green. They look almost catlike, but he's no feline shifter. I halt, still staring at his eyes.

"Are you afraid?" I ask.

He pales and doesn't answer.

I grin. The big, pain-in-the-ass man has a weakness, and I'm onto it. "Are you claustrophobic?" I ask.

He glares at me. All his arrogance has vanished, and it's making him seem more human, as real as anybody else.

"I don't like tight places. My beast is wary of them."

I suppress a laugh. "Sorry, but this is not a sight-seeing tour. I'm sure they have something during daylight hours that may suit your space requirement."

Other than his growl, silence is my only answer.

A moment later, I catch a glimmer of light in the distance. "Maybe you were listening, it seems that we found light at the end of that tunnel," I say and continue to walk sideways as he follows me.

I know by the pull that I'm on the right path. I'm getting closer to my mission's purpose. Excitement grows, and it's like I've suddenly grown wings that make me advance faster.

At the end of the narrow path, the walls and ceiling suddenly disappear and we're left in a space so dizzyingly vast that I almost fall. He grabs my hand and steadies me. I peer down from the edge and see trees below. How and why are they growing *inside* the cave?

A chill runs down my spine, and I scan the area.

A group of ghosts are down there – and they seem to be reliving their last moments.

"Ah, fuck!"

Drake looks at me. "What?"

I take a deep breath. "You don't want to know."

LILANDRA

I received a call... but it is weird.

I thought I'd lost that relic a decade ago – the mere memory of it is enough to make me tear up, because my mate died on that mission. What is the meaning of this? Why is the ring back from its evil hiding place and calling to me again?

In honor of my mate's memory, I am finishing what I started, even though it won't bring him back. At least I will have the satisfaction of closing a chapter of my life. Maybe, just maybe, I'll be able to move on.

The corridor is dark, but I hear a crack somewhere in the vicinity.

I cast a spell to surround myself with different kinds of magical guns.

"Who's there?" My gut tells me I'm not alone. "Show yourself."

A Fae steps out of hiding, holding her hands up. "Sorry, I didn't mean to startle you," she says.

I regard her. "A Fae? What are *you* doing here?" I don't see them often, even in the neutral zone. Their community is close to ours, but most of the time, they keep to themselves.

She grimaces. "I will tell you, but can you lower your weapons?"

I reduce the number of guns at my disposal, but keep a couple just in case.

"I asked for all," she says.

I shrug. "Sorry that I didn't comply, but you didn't give me a good enough reason. So, can we talk now?"

She lowers her hands. "I am unarmed. I'm not here to start a fight, Witch Warrior."

"What are you here for, then, and who are you?"

She takes a deep breath. "My name is Maria."

"A Fae called Maria."

"No, but Maria is the name I use when I'm interacting with humans or other species. You will not be able to pronounce my real one."

I smile, amused by her. "I am Lilandra. Why are you following me?"

"I'm not following you, but since you found a way in here when I couldn't, I made myself almost invisible. I'm part of the Faeries Internal Affair agency, and I'm on a mission."

I squint at her. "What kind of mission?"

"Gathering intelligence."

"And what did you gather? "

She gives me a tight-lipped smile. "We have some disturbing news. There's a group, formed by individuals across different species, working against the faction system. They are here, looking for something. I don't know what, but I know it's big."

I stay silent. I know something's going on right now. Everybody knows it. We can't hide the fact. We've had a lot of intel about it, but we don't have any clue about the real perpetrator or the motivation behind all this.

"We got the same thing. Supernatural Intelligence Agency are working on the case, too. Not only the witches, but Vampire Internal Affair is, too. I don't know yet for the were-wolf part, but we are all expecting something big."

Maria stays silent a moment. Then she asks, "You're on a mission right now?"

"Yes."

"Do you mind if I tag along? I may be able to help you, and that might help me to gather information."

I make all my guns disappear.

She starts to breathe easier once more.

"Maybe you can. We're looking for an old artifact that I lost a decade ago. It's calling to me again."

She nods at me. "Great. I will follow you."

I walk ahead toward the relic that pulls at my internal magic sense.

As we go, I study my new ally, for now. It's odd running into someone else here, so I'll keep my guard up. You never know when a faerie can turn against you.

CHAPTER EIGHT

THE LADY

Selena rushes into my office. "My Lady, we lost contact with the group. They entered the magic cave, but it's radio silence in there."

I glance at my watch and calculate the time difference. It's around three am there. "Could we have planned for this?"

"We don't know all the magical traps and other things that are inside that cave. They were lucky to have the ring. Without it, I suspect they still wouldn't have made their way inside."

It's morning here. Now time doesn't have any grip on them. "For them, time stops: they'll have no way to know the difference between day and night. Lucky for them, Jeremy is with them. A vampire needs his beauty sleep, even if it's just a couple of hours."

"I agree with you, my Lady. Now we have to wait."

"I'm not good at waiting. In this case, I have no choice. Do we know if our enemies have entered the cave?"

Selena consults her pad. She swipes through the different

reports she receives from the spies we have close to our team on missions. We need to have eyes and ears everywhere.

"We know about Juniper. But Lilandra is reported to be there, too."

"What? Why?"

"Sorry, my Lady, but I suspect the ring called her."

I want to slap myself. I didn't plan for this, but I should've anticipated it: Lilandra is a Witch Warrior and specializing in jewelry. "You said she's there too, but did she enter the way Juniper did?"

"We started to map all the entrances. We believe there are many entrances to that cave. Some could be dead ends or traps, but there's no way to know for sure."

"We can only hope for the best. My instinct told me to send them reinforcement. Prepare another team to be there if they escape and need back up."

Selena nods and her fingers fly over her pad. "Ordered. Now, we have no choice but to wait."

That stone is integral to my success. If Lilandra is there for the ring, the team needs to be very careful. Now they have two Witch Warriors to fight.

~

JUNIPER

I give up.

For now, we continue on the narrow path, but I'm starting to wish that the corridor was a little wider. The walls are closing in on us, and, now, a different feeling comes over me. As we go on, I have more space. The farther we walk, we are able to walk normally, one behind the other. My breaths come easier.

"Oh, that's one tight corridor if you ask me. I hope that we don't encounter another," he says.

I study him. He's not so pale anymore, and his cockiness is back in full force. Clearly, close quarters rattled him more than he'd like to admit.

"You never know in places like these. Traps or other magic tricks could be closer than we think. We need to be on guard, just in case." I don't want him to think I care for him. I'm simply saying the truth. The pull towards the right is still strong, but now there's another, telling me there's something for me on my left, too.

He notices. "What is it?"

"The object I'm looking for is on the path to the right, but something familiar is down the left one."

A clatter echoes through the tunnel.

He flinches, and his gaze darts from place to place. "I see two women. One human, probably a witch like you, but the other is a faerie."

"Do you see anything more? Is the Witch Warrior a hostage?" Another clue for me: his eyesight is superb.

"Go on." I push him to tell me more and draw out my katana. I have to wait. If a faerie is there, that can only mean there are more factions involved with the secret society.

"No, they are talking. They are coming this way, and the Witch Warrior is looking in our direction."

So the Witch Warrior knows I'm here. Could she be a traitor? I take a deep breath through my nose, and take in a familiar scent.

He frowns.

"No way!" I yell, rushing ahead.

He tells me to stop, that it could be dangerous, but I'm not listening. If my magic is right, it only means one thing. I run as fast as I can until I see her.

She's here.

"Lilandra!" I scream.

She smiles at me. Her faerie friend looks taken aback as I slam into Lilandra and wrap my arms around her. It's that good to see her.

"I didn't think you even went on missions anymore," I tell her, so excited that it's hard for me to keep from blabbing.

"Slow down, little one," she says. "I know you have questions. I can see them all over your face. Take a deep breath."

I do what my mentor tells me. My magic is always a little crazy when I see her. "So, what are you doing here?" I point to the faerie. "And who is she?"

Lilandra gestures behind me. "I could ask the same about him."

I turn around. I totally forgot about him. "Don't mind him. He decided to be my shadow, but I don't know why."

"What are your instincts telling you?" Lilandra asks me.

"That I am supposed to turn right where the paths diverge, and you?"

"Same for me."

"That means that our objects are close to one another."

"Care to explain what's going on?" the faerie asks.

I figure by her tone and the way she stands, she's annoyed.

Lilandra nods. "This is Marie. Well, that's what she tells me to call her because we will not be able to pronounce her real fae name. This is Juniper. She's my mentee and one of the strongest Witch Warriors that we have." She looks expectantly at Drake. "And you are?"

"My name is Drake. I follow her, since without me she'd be wounded or dead. I think you already know that I'm a shifter."

Lilandra nods. "Yes, but which kind? I've never encountered one like you."

He smiles but doesn't answer.

"Don't even try," I say. "I did without success. He is extremely annoying, so just ignore him like I do."

Lilandra chuckles. "I'm sorry, Drake, for her poor manners, but she developed them despite my best efforts."

"Hey!" I bark, mad at both of them.

All of them start to laugh.

"We can take a little break and talk at the next crossroads. I need something to eat. Did you bring anything?" Lilandra asks.

"My manners may be lacking, but I know how to get the job done and what to bring on these missions. Especially when we don't know how long we could be stuck somewhere. We'll have to find another exit point since the one that we used has collapsed."

Lilandra shakes her head. "What did you do this time?"

"Me? Nothing. That was his fault."

He makes a noise behind me. "If that wasn't for me, you would be dead. Don't forget it."

"Yeah, yeah. Anyway. We need to go to the right. Do you feel you're on the same path, Lilandra?"

She nods. "Yes, but it seems far at the same time. Does your pull feel the same?"

I close my eyes and concentrate on the stone. It's close and urges me to go faster. "The only thing that I can say is that the stone is afraid and wants me to hurry."

Lilandra gathers kindling to help create a fire. *"Ignis!"*

A fire appears, and we take seats around it. "Let's eat and relax. You said you arrived in the middle of the night. What time could it be now?"

"Probably closer to the morning. I'm pretty sure the sun is rising right now. We have to discuss all this. And I want to know more about you, Marie. What is a faerie doing here?"

She looks at me. Next to us, she seems so fragile, but appearances can be deceiving: my species studies have taught me that faeries are more than capable of holding their own in a fight. She could be a badass.

Lilandra puts food over the fire and cooks for us. I brought another bag filled with enough food for all of us, including water.

We need to know more, but the jolt inside me puts me on edge. I can feel the stone's fear, and our enemies must know that I'm here to help it.

~

DONOVAN

We just escaped a magical trap. That was close. The scent of trees and grass comes from in front of us.

"What is it, love?" Sophia asks me.

"I'm smelling grass and trees at the end of this tunnel."

She casts a healing spell to help me heal faster from the injuries I sustained before we escaped the last trap. "How is that possible?"

"Anything is possible, my love. I know in my magic and my bones that this place was magically created by a powerful entity. I'm not sure, but I think that entity is still alive, because no known magic can survive that long." I give her a quick kiss on her lips.

I turn to Jeremy. "Are you okay?"

He yawns as his eyes are glazing over. "My body is demanding sleep – it's probably day outside. Lucky that I am affected less since we are in these caves. I need to lay down and have a 'power nap,' as humans call it."

The light at the end of the tunnel looms close. I'm able to feel and smell the wind. "Can you hold on until we're out of these tight quarters? My wolf is becoming erratic."

Jeremy nods at me. "Just hope there's no sun there, or I will have to stay inside the cave until the sun is down."

We continue forward and enter a forest inside a cave.

I study the changing sky. It's daylight, and I turn to Jeremy.

He shrugs. "No effect. It's the magical light, but it's not ultraviolet like the real sun. This is only an image."

As I watch, he looks at the sky, but he doesn't bother about the surroundings. He must have never seen the sun like this, being a pureblood. "I almost stayed where I was. I was afraid it would have the same effect on me as the sun does."

"It appears to have no effect on you," I say.

"It's magic. It's like a light inside of a house. Probably to help the plants and trees grow," Jeremy tells us, looking over his skin for any signs of damage.

Jeremy finds a place to sit and be comfortable. We gather close to him, and we relax a little. I consider the ring in my skin that lets me feel the stone close to us.

"This magic is very powerful. I don't know who is casting it, but I'm sure that it takes a lot of energy to keep a place like this."

I sit on the ground with the others, and Sophia sits in my lap. Lucas pulls Grace onto his lap too.

"This is a wolf thing, right?" Sophia asks me with a smirk.

"Maybe... or maybe I just don't want your dress to get dirty," I say.

She laughs. "So, what's next?"

"Well, our vampire here needs his beauty sleep. We've got no choice but to give it to him. After he wakes, I hope he doesn't need to drink."

"I don't think so. Jeremy fed before we left. Since he's older, he can go without eating for days."

I look up. The sun and the trees look so real that I could

almost believe we're outside. "Do you think that magic follows outside path?"

Sophia follows my gaze. "Maybe, not sure but it is a possibility. I know in my magic that whoever cast this spell is still alive. Which means it is very old."

I stay still as Sophia tries to figure it all out. The mission is already unusual, but we need to succeed if we want freedom from those ancient faction rules that are keeping us from the life we want.

$$\sim$$

LILANDRA

I breathe.

The ring that cost me my mate is here, and calling me again. My next breath takes away the anguish.

Juniper is here, too. I breathe the excitement and anticipation away.

Sophia contacted me some time ago. I give the dread and hurt to my breath and clear my mind of all thoughts.

I've lost track of time, with all these non-stop missions.

"Can you trust faeries?"

I smile at Juniper's question. She was always slow to trust. I'm surprised she even let Drake follow her. "I can ask you the same about the shifter. His secrecy could be a trick."

Juniper looks at him. "Maybe. I know what needs to be done. The priority is the magical object."

The first rule of being a Witch Warrior. The top priority is the magical object.

I can sense that her nerves are on edge. She can control a part of it, but the rest will only come with age. "You need to rein yourself in. Being on edge all the time is not good for you."

She chuckles. "Well. Maybe later, or never. I'd rather be on edge. That way, I'm always prepared for the worst."

She never removes her katana or her guns while on a mission. My weapons are easy. They are part of my magic and they are always there. For Juniper, it's different. Her casting is the fastest in the coven. She can change bullet type within a few fractions of a second. That's how fast she is. Not only is she skilled in hand to hand combat, she can manipulate her katana the same way and add magic to it.

"You still have your katana?" I ask.

She takes it out of its sheath. "Yes, it belonged to my father. From what I understand, the katana is very old and has always been a part of my family of witch warriors."

I recall the first time I saw her. I didn't understand why the great Witch Warrior Council assigned me to her, since we don't have the same kind of calling. With time, I understood, but it's not the time to be sentimental. We have a mission, and we are stuck underground in a place that is full of magical traps.

"We've got a job to do. That's the priority."

CHAPTER NINE

DONOVAN

I LOOK AT MY TEAM. I CAN FEEL THE RING IN MY SKIN. IT'S like a tracking device. Werewolves are magical creatures, but I never understood that kind of magic power. The energy that some can control, like my mate. In my book, that's too much power for one person, and yet there are others even more powerful than her.

"What is it, love?" I smile at her. Our bond has strengthened over time. Since we're in close proximity to each other, the link is even more intense. Sophia touches the tree in front of us. "Just think of what kind of magic you need to create all this can bind on some other that could do worse."

She doesn't reply to my comment. She knows that I love her; she's my mate for life. We continue to walk. The demon is in front of us. They have a better sense of smell than werewolves – unfair, if you ask me, but it's the truth. The forest is so big, and its tallest trees have been growing for centuries.

"Nice to walk in the light, huh, Jeremy?" I call out to the

vampire. "Now you can enjoy it. Other vampires would be so jealous if they knew."

He smiles like a kid.

Sophia shakes her head but she's got a smug look on her face.

"Why he is grinning like that?" The demon asks me in his deep and rough voice.

I shrug. "Vampires never go when the sun is up. They die if they try. Since he is a pureblood, meaning he was born a vampire, he never experienced the sun before. Vampires turned from humans know it. He never has."

The demon nods at me. The he freezes and waves his hand. "Hide, everyone."

All of us stop and hide in the bush.

"What?" I mouth at him.

"We are not alone," he says in a hoarse whisper.

I scan the area, then close my eyes to call my wolf to help me, but I can't smell anything, and neither does my wolf. "Are you sure?"

"Positive. They are at the opposite end of the forest. They must have come from another entrance."

Who's here with us? Are they friend or foe?

I squint at the spaces between the trees. "Can you tell me what they are?"

"Not yet. I just know there's four of them. What they are, I can't tell."

I nod. We know for certain now that we are not alone, but they may not know that we are here, so we may still have an advantage over them.

"We keep quiet. They may be far. Since we don't know what we are dealing with yet, we'll stay cautious," I tell them.

We move again, but more carefully. Why can't a mission ever be simple? We don't need to draw any more attention to ourselves.

The demon points in the direction that the other group is coming from. They could be reinforcements: that's the way the Lady works. If that's the case, the more, the better.

I consider my group, my brothers and sisters in arms. We need to succeed. The ring pulls me in its direction. I glance at Sophia.

She smiles and kisses me briefly. "We will succeed, love. I have faith in us."

"We don't know if they are more than four. There could be more."

She nods and takes my hand. The proximity of the stone makes me more on edge with that ring embedded in my skin. My wolf is not happy: he's running wild inside my head. I don't know if it is because of the ring or because we're so close to completing our mission. One thing is for sure, we will fight.

No matter who we are up against.

~

JUNIPER

We don't talk much.

The tree line of a big forest starts just ahead of us, and the sky seems to mirror the conditions outside. It would take a massive amount of magic energy to create and sustain something like this underground. How many years, if not centuries, has this forest been here?

"What do you think?"

I glance at my mentor. "Creating and maintaining a simulation of the sky outside is a huge energy expense. Who would be able to do all this?"

Lilandra touches one of the trees in front of us. "These are not magic. Only the sky and the weather are. The sun doesn't have the same property as ours outside. Plants need ultraviolet light to grow, but the magic must be supplying it somehow."

I caress one of the leaves. It looks, smells and feels exactly the same as any other leaf from above ground. But the rest is all created by spells and magic, and the one who originally cast it must still be alive today, because as long as they draw breath, their magic survives..

"What is it?" Marie asks us.

Drake tips his head to the side as he peers at me. He sniffs the air. "The smell of everything is real, but something is not entirely normal."

"True, Drake. It's a magic creation, but why is it here, and who put it there?"

When we start moving again, I walk beside Lilandra. "So, what are we going to do about Drake and Marie?"

She looks at me in surprise. "Well, for now, nothing. They're helping us. Which is great, if you ask me. We don't know what we might be up against. I got a sixth sense that tells me we're not alone here." She pushes a few branches aside so we can pass.

"Maybe. But that also means we don't know if they are with us."

Lilandra chuckles. "Always wondering when people will turn against you, I see."

She's right: it's a bad habit of mine, but it's kept me alive until now. "You know me. I'd rather be on my guard and ready. We can't trust them."

"I can't say much about the faeries, and you don't have any information about Drake either. You can't make that decision yet, but you keep him beside you anyway."

"You have a point." I don't want to admit it to her, but for some reason, the stone is calling me to hurry. It senses the enemy is close to it.

"Less talking, more walking," she says.

I turn to look at Drake. His eyes have changed, but not like a werewolf's would.

"We are not alone," he offers.

I try to scan inside the forest. "What do you mean that we're not alone?"

His eyes are normal once more. "There are at least six people in our path. I suspect they are going for the stone, too."

"What are they?"

"Two shifters, two witches, one vampire and one demon," Drake tells us calmly.

"A demon? Are you sure?" Demons never work outside of their clan, and they have to travel here from other realms.

He moves closer to me. "You doubt what I tell you. You can't see them, but I don't know if they can already see us. Demons have very good eyesight."

"Better than you and the werewolves?"

"Yes, way better."

"Vision scelerisque!"

I look at Lilandra. Her eyes change. She's the only witch that could call anything that help her in her mission. Her magic is so much more powerful. She tells me that I'm the strongest of the Witch Warriors, but I think she is. She doesn't have any weapons – she creates what she needs with only her magic.

"I see them," she says.

"Can you tell us who they are?"

Lilandra lets out a deep sigh. "Oh, dear, not them."

"Who?" I ask.

"Donovan and his team. He has three with him that I can't recognize."

"Meaning?"

"Well, Drake, is right – they have a demon with them, but

there's also another werewolf and another witch. I think she's an earth one."

She stops her vision spell, and her eyes return to normal.

"The three others are Donovan, his mate, and that vampire, right?" I ask.

She nods.

Great. Now we have not *three* but *six* to fight against, and there's only four of us. "The pull is strong, Lilandra," I say. "That stone is very close to us."

"I know. I feel the pull, also. The ring is close. I just wonder where it is."

We each scan the area. I don't see the others, but I trust Lilandra's assessment. It means only one thing: this mission has just become much more difficult.

I peer into the shadows between the tree trunks. Where are they? How come they were closer to the stone? They don't have a Witch Warrior or anything of magic to help lead them, but it definitely seems like they know where the stone is. This is not good.

"We have no choice. We need to get to the stone first."

I take in Lilandra and the rest of the group. "That's the only solution. We must try to avoid a fight with them. The space here is limited for our magic."

"We have no choice, right?" Drake says.

"True, but not knowing precisely where the stone is makes it seem that a fight against them will be inevitable."

I try to focus on that stone. I need a signal or something that will help me find its exact location. It could be on the ground level, but it could also be underground. Drake takes my hand and meets my gaze. I'm not removing his hand from mine, and, even as I'm wondering why, he smiles at me. Why his damn dimples have that effect on me, I'll never know.

He leans closer, and I turn to say something to him. But

he crashes his lips to mine and takes full advantage of the fact that my mouth is wide open. His tongue meets mine, circling.

Never in my life have I felt anything like this. *Why* is he kissing me?

~

THE LADY

Almost twenty-four hours passed. Still no contact from them.

"My Lady?"

I look at Selena. My most loyal follower, she has no idea what I have in store for her. The day I proceed with the plan will be a sad one.

"Yes, Selena?"

"We still don't have any news, but the second team just arrived. They're struggling with opening the door to the cave. Do you think the ring made it easier for Donovan's group?"

Ancient relics are complicated sometimes. They're as finicky as a persnickety grandmother. We never know how their magic works. Some of the objects are very old, and only the people with suitable magic energy could hope to ever learn how to work them..

"It's still daylight out there. They will need to wait until nightfall. Those doors are the easiest to open since they are there to prevent humans from venturing inside."

Selena nods. In Scotland, it is right in the middle of the afternoon, but here it's only late morning.

"Tell them to wait at Donovan's last known coordinates as backup. "

Selena starts texting – I assume she's relaying my orders. I need that backup team down there in case something happens. With Witch Warriors around, it almost certainly will. I wish they didn't exist, but making that happen is one of my goals.

"My Lady?"

"Yes, Selena?"

"The backup team will wait for nightfall to try and enter the cave, but is there any way for us to help them do it?"

"No – if they fail, they will have to wait until the door opens again. Hopefully they'll be able to join the other team."

She nods, and leaves me in my office. I pinch the bridge of my nose and look at my hand – I never liked dark colors, but it's not like I have a choice now. I want everything to be an advantage, to make them pay for what they did to me.

I sigh. Life was easy in the past, but now? My wish for revenge drives me, my desire to get back at those who exiled me to a place where I almost lost my soul. They will feel the pain I suffered through – only then will I be at peace with my past.

They won't know what hit them.

CHAPTER TEN

JUNIPER

I SLAP HIM. *HARD.* "YOU SON OF A BITCH! DON'T touch me."

My outburst echoes through the tunnel. Lilandra and Marie turn to stare at us. My handprint appears like an angry red welt on his face. Ever so slowly, he strokes his face as his shocked expression morphs into a cocky smile.

That fucker.

Lilandra's voice brings me back to my senses. "Stop it, Juniper. You will blow our cover."

That bastard made me forget about our mission and the precarious position we're in. My palm is pulsing from the blow I delivered – it was hard enough to knock out a regular man or even any other kind of paranormal creature, but he's just standing there, smirking at me as the outline of my hand colors his cheek.

"Juniper, focus."

I glare at my mentor, then point at him. I'm ready to kill right now. "You stay out of my way."

He doesn't budge.

"Drake, if you pull anything like this again, she *will* kill you," Lilandra says.

He chuckles. "I don't think so."

I have so many questions, but no answers about him. I wish we weren't in this place, and that I had the spare time to interrogate him with my magic. I would make him tell me everything.

I take a breath. The only way I can focus my anger is by meditation, but the weight of Halloween approaching is making my magic more difficult to control. I glance back at Lilandra. Marie looks to be enjoying the show. Sure, Drake's manners need a lot of improvement, but I need to gain control, to let go of my anger. I don't give anyone the right to touch me without my consent.

I look toward where the enemies should be. I don't know if they can see us. But judging by the way they're creeping toward us, they probably already know we are here.

"They're getting closer. I get the feeling they know we are here," Marie tells us.

I draw out my katana and grasp my gun with the other hand. Lilandra casts her regular weapon spell. We have no choice but to fight: they are in our way.

We need them gone so we can bring back both magical items that have called for our protection.

"I'm taking the demon," Drake yells. Without warning, he bolts out of our hiding place.

"*Argenti,*" I whisper to my gun, and the bullets turn into silver ones. "I'm taking the werewolf and the witches."

"No, Donovan's mate is mine."

I look at Lilandra. "Why?"

"I don't have to tell you why." Lilandra rushes toward Donovan and the witch beside him. That leaves the other werewolf, another witch, and the vampire.

Marie swings a long sword. I don't know where it came from.

"I'm taking the vampire," she says. "You know what you have to do."

Shit. Like I don't know what that leaves for me. I burst into the fray. Drake is already engaged in his battle with the demon, and I worry.

Stop, Juniper. He can do it. You already see it.

"So, you're the little bitch that's against us." I don't recognize the werewolf snarling at me. The witch starts to cast, and the ground beneath us shifts.

Oh, great. Lilandra was right: an earth witch.

"You want some silver, dog?" I scream.

Halfway transformed, he charges me. How I love fighting them! Weres not only challenge me magically, but physically as well. I squeeze the trigger repeatedly, but each time my bullet flies true, the witch blocks it with an earth wall.

"Ignis," I whisper to my katana. A bright flame ignites over the blade.

The beast wants me to drop my weapon – he doesn't know he's in for a ride if he engages in hand to hand combat. I run towards him, inching closer, still peppering him with silver bullets, but the witch sends stones to block them.

"You're dead, Witch Warrior," he says with a growl.

"In your dreams, dog."

He chuckles and then fully transforms into his werewolf form. I launch a kick at him, but he dodges, way faster than any werewolf I ever fought. He's on speed or something. No way his witch could be helping with that. It's not a part of her magic.

I feint a kick, and when he dodges, he winds up right where I want him. I land a spinning back kick directly to his face, and he yelps.

"Lucas!" the witch screams at him.

I head toward her, confident that my direct face hit will slow him down. I need to take her out of commission. It's the only way I can beat the werewolf on my own.

"Stop now, Juniper!" I turn around and see that Donovan and the witch have Lilandra in their clutches.

Breath catches in my throat. No way. It's impossible.

"You stop now or I kill your mentor."

I look at Lilandra. Something in her eyes makes me stop, but I don't put my katana or my gun down. Drake is still fighting that demon and Marie is busy with the vampire.

My weapons have to be at the ready. Donnovan and his witch are close enough for me to do something to free my mentor. But a shadow in Lilandra's eyes makes me rethink what I want to do. She's given into them. It's not normal. Not for Lilandra.

Our first rule: the call must be the answer and the magical object brought back at all costs. Even if we need to die to make it happen. We *never* submit.

Lilandra has my complete attention. I get the feeling that she will need back up for something she has planned, but what?

DONOVAN

Now that my beautiful mate has Lilandra at her mercy, Juniper has to surrender. The two of them exchange looks. Lilandra was surprisingly easy to capture, being allegedly one of the best Witch Warriors – clearly, the next generation has surpassed the old guard.

"Free her now, or there will be hell to pay." Juniper's dark blue eyes flash as if she's trying to singe me on the spot.

"Lay down your weapon."

She smirks at us. "You don't know me well enough. You won't be safe until you free my mentor. Now." She gestures with her gun and her katana.

"Love, she's got a silver spell in her weapon. Careful," Sophia cautions. "Juniper, don't push my mate. He is the pack alpha, stronger than any werewolf."

She laughs in our faces.

Oh, that bitch. I thought Lilandra was the worst cynic, but that was before I met Juniper.

Juniper holsters her gun and twirls her katana. "Something tells me that you will be the losers here. You better surrender. If you do, they'll let you stay together in Supernatural Intelligence Agency cells as they interrogate you. You must cooperate with us."

My wolf growls. He doesn't like Juniper. Not only is she defiant, but she wants to challenge me, the alpha. "Dream on, little girl."

She looks from her mentor to me. Anger burns in her eyes. "This little girl will kick your ass so hard, you and your wolf will remember me for a long time."

My wolf accepts her challenge, and I bare my teeth, snarling.

She waves her katana around in a complicated move.

"She removed her silver spell. No magic on it," Sophia whispers, nodding towards Juniper's katana.

It's a ballsy challenge that I can't ignore. I undo my shirt and toss it aside, transforming half-way so that I resemble a werewolf on two feet. It will be an advantage. However, it will cost me a lot of stamina to stay half-changed like this.

"You're scared to show me your dog?"

I growl at her comment. My teeth are all out, and I bite at the air.

"Careful," Sophia whispers.

I lunge at Juniper, but she dodges me easily. Maybe she really is the best Witch Warrior.

She whirls toward me. "I'm not going to cast, dog. So come and get me."

I run into the trees, hoping they will obscure me from Juniper's vision. I want to surprise her, but it doesn't seem possible. I continue on the same path, but, at the last moment, I jump up and bounce off a tree trunk, adding more strength and speed to my charge. As I sail through the air toward Juniper, something cuts my skin, alighting it with blistering pain.

But I haven't even reached the witch. What is happening? I look down to see a spell slicing my skin where Sophia embedded the ring.

"That ring doesn't belong to you. It's calling to me," Lilandra says.

I have no idea how to stop what Lilandra is doing to me. The magic cooks my skin, and the smell of burned flesh wafts through the air. Where's Sophia? I search for my mate. Horror freezes me where I stand when I see her on the floor, unconscious.

Is she dead? The question nearly knocks me back.

The ring leaves my body, leaving only a flap of skin behind. Blood pours down my chest, but I rush to Sophia's side.

"The ring belongs to me. Leave us. Before it's too late for all of you," Lilandra warns.

At that, I howl to my beta, still limping toward my mate. Nothing matters now. Nothing except *her*. Her scent reaches me, warm and familiar. She's alive. Relief floods me.

I return to human form and take her in my arms. Lucas retreats closer to me.

I need to hide my mate. I must protect her at all costs.

~

DRAKE

I've fought a demon twice now... for my mate. She's so beautiful when she's fighting.

"Demon, get back where you belong. This is not your realm."

He swings at me, but I dodge the punch easily.

"You need to go and leave us to do the Lady's bidding." The demon said in a gravelly voice.

"The Lady? Who is the Lady?"

"You have no chance against all of us. We are many, and powerful."

That's new information, and might be important for my mate's mission. I grab the demon's wrist and wrench him closer, then begin to twist it. "Tell me more, demon. Who is this Lady of yours?"

He tries to jab me with his other hand, but I snap the arm I'm holding in two, and he bellows in pain.

"Now, are you ready to talk?" I ask.

Pain resides in his dark eyes. "No one can go against us." He grunts. "What are you?" he dares to ask.

"I'll never tell. That secret belongs to me and me only." I strike him as hard as I can. My mate needs me. The feeling curls through my mind.

The faerie struggles against the vampire, who has summoned small dark faeries. Those are rare , and if they themselves to someone, they will execute his every order.

As my mate fights a werewolf, Lilandra gets herself captured.

I smile. Life with my mate is going to be full of surprises.

~

LILANDRA

This victory is most bitter. I study the object I lost a decade ago. I sacrificed my other half to obtain it, and I never found another mate.

I let Donovan and Sophia go. I know what it means to lose a fated mate. I wouldn't wish it on anyone.

"Why are you letting them go? They'll be back."

I glance at my fired-up mentee, all desire to fight hand to hand to the death. "Thanks for the distraction. I needed it."

She sighs.

My mission is over. Priorities are priorities. Now I can help Juniper complete hers, too. Working together, we will be back to the coven sooner.

"That's what you were trying to tell me?" she asks.

"Yes, but, like usual, you did more than we needed. You enjoy the fight."

She smiles.

I know her very well. Too well, perhaps.

"It's always fun to have a good fight without magic."

"One day, Juniper, that will be your doom."

"I'm too stubborn to die."

That's what I thought when I was her age, but life made me harder, taught me that there were fates worse than death. "I don't want you to die before me, you know."

She tips her head to the side. "That's why you let them capture you?"

"I needed to obtain the relic. I knew that they had it, but I didn't know where it was. Everything pointed to Donovan, but I didn't know where. When he removed his shirt, I saw it embedded beneath his skin. It was the item we fought for, and we didn't want to lose it."

My best friend turned enemy leaves in the arms of her mate. I know she's alive and breathing; I only knocked her out. She may be one of the more powerful fire witches, but she has no skills in a fight.

"We will see them very soon," I say. "They will not leave until they find the stone that you're looking for."

Juniper sighs. "You're right." She looks around. "It's very close. I'm sure Donovan knows that, too."

I turn around in time to see Drake snapping the demon's arms in two. Then he let it go.

"So you got your fun," he tells Juniper.

She doesn't answer. I suspect they have something going on, but it's difficult to know for sure with Juniper.

"You got the ring?" Marie asks.

"Yes, lucky that Juniper provided me with a diversion, so I was able to draw it out."

The light in the dome shifts slowly toward darkness. "Night is coming. We need to heal get some sleep, and find the stone. Then we need to get out of here, because they will be back," I tell them.

We choose a place close to a grove of trees. The thicket below gives us some protection.

"I'm taking the guard shift," Drake announces.

"We'll call you if we need you. I suspect the night will be quiet, but that's probably not going to be the case tomorrow morning."

I let Drake gather wood to make a fire.

We won this round, but we're vulnerable until we get back to the coven.

CHAPTER ELEVEN

DONOVAN

"SHIT. THAT HURTS!" I KNOW THAT WOUNDS AREN'T LIFE-threatening, but they're painful.

"Please, love, stay calm until I finish," Sophia says.

I smile at her. She always heals me, though a werewolf can heal quickly on its own. Even faster if their mate is with them.

"Still think she's your best friend, love?" I ask.

She glares at me. Well, maybe I'm in more trouble. I just need to shut up sometimes.

"You're stupid, you know that, love?"

I harden my expression, and my muscles work in my jaw.

"You're aware that if she wanted to kill either of us, she could have ? But she didn't.."

I close my eyes and rub my forehead. "Really? That's what you think? That she's still your best friend, and that she will help us? Sorry to tell you, love, but she declined the perfect gift she could have had when she brought the Seal of Solomon to the coven."

My mate has a bit of a blind spot when it comes to Lilandra.

"You know nothing," Sophia says, anger flashing in her gorgeous eyes. "Lilandra's powers could have transformed her fingernails to knives to kill you on the spot. She didn't. She only reclaimed that damned ring, which is what made her lose her mate at the end."

The darkness deepens, and I turn away from Sophia.

"We need to build a fire. How is everybody?" I turn to my team. Some are cut and bruised, but they are all alive. "Jeremy, do you need sleep? Or blood?" I know, eventually, he will need some. How he's going to get it is not a question I'm ready to ask yet.

"A few hours would be good," he answers. "And don't worry. We still have a few days before my thirst comes back."

It's great to have a vampire in our group. They need less sleep than the rest of us. He's been up for almost twenty-four hours straight. We're lucky that he's not affected by this sunlight and weather spell.

"I wonder, alpha, what would happen to him if the sun was up? What would he do?" Lucas asks.

I don't know the answer, so we all look to Jeremy.

Jeremy laughs. "Well, easy, we dig a hole. Then we stay in the ground until the sun goes down." Then Jeremy climbs to his feet and goes across the camp. He sits down with his back against a tree. Within seconds, he's asleep.

I turn to the demon. "What about you? Are you fine?"

He snarls. "I will be. We heal fast, too." He speaks in a gravelly voice, a holdover from the underworld. "That guy I fought is insanely strong – some kind of shifter.."

"We'll figure it out eventually. Now we rest. They need rest also. Tomorrow, we will continue our mission. The stone is our priority, but if we are able to snatch the ring back, that will be the icing on the cake."

I draw my mate into an embrace and snuggle with her. She puts her head on my chest, her ear resting just above my heart, kisses my skin, and then falls asleep. I know our enemies will not come tonight. If they had, I would already smell them.

Tomorrow will come soon enough, and we'll need to find that stone quickly.

~

JUNIPER

Half of me is still wired from the fight, but the other half wants to sleep.

Drake watches over us. That man is a mystery. I have no answers for the questions swirling in my mind. He can take on a demon by himself and come out on top without a single scratch. Few in the paranormal community could beat a demon like that, and no ordinary shifter can.

At least that's what I learned in my studies: the only one that can resist a demon is a pureblood vampire with a belly full of blood.

I shift in place, rolling over to observe my teacher. Lilandra has been my mentor for so many years. Her fated mate has been dead for a decade now, and she decided to make mentorship her life's purpose. I thought I knew all about her, but I can sense a secret between us. She conjures a spell, an enchantment that helps people heal in their sleep, and lays it over us. Then she adds some incense to the fire. A pleasant, calming scent fills the air.

Slowly, my eyes close. Halloween draws nearer, and the pull of the stone is starting to drive me nuts. It's a thorn in my side.

On the other side of the fire, Lilandra continues her casting. Marie is fully asleep, and I am not far from it. My eyes are closing by themselves. The last thing I see is Lilandra talking to Drake. Yet even my curiosity doesn't prevent me from venturing into the land of dreams.

~

LILANDRA

"What did you do?" Drake scoots closer to me.

I grin. "They need to sleep. Both were wounded, and Juniper needs her rest since Halloween is right around the corner. She won't be getting much sleep over the next forty-eight hours."

He takes a seat beside me.

I point to his body. "I see that you've healed perfectly."

He flexes his arm and then his chest. "That demon is nothing against me." He seems very proud of himself.

"You're not going to tell us what you are, are you?" I study him. I want to understand his non-verbal cues. I need to know more. Through my magic, I can sense that his energy is in tune with Juniper's. A suspicion comes to me, but I keep it to myself.

"No. She'll learn one day, but now is not the time." He takes a handful of twigs and places them on the fire. Sparks fill the air.

"You know that if you hurt her, I will kill you," I say.

His gaze cuts to me. He seems amused. "I know you're telling the truth, but believe me, that's not why I'm here. Quite the opposite. I'm here to protect her."

"Juniper can protect herself. She's been trained for that."

He chuckles again. "I know, but that doesn't mean she can't get hurt, especially being as reckless as she is. I'm here to prevent that. She doesn't value her life enough." He stares at the fire like the flame mesmerizes him.

"I sense that you got a very strong affinity for fire."

"True."

"How come?" I ask.

"Nice try, but Juniper will be the first to know. Until she knows, nobody else can know. Including you."

I take a deep breath and close my eyes. The incense calms me, but now that I have the ring back, I can move on from everything that happened last night. I can finally close the chapter that haunts me: the night that my joy died, causing only despair to rule in my heart.

When I open my eyes, Drake is staring at me with a weird look on his face. "What?"

"I thought you fell asleep."

I laugh. "Meditation can look like sleep. It's a form of rest."

"Well, that was a long meditation. That wasn't a quick blink," he answers.

"True, but meditation, for us, most of the time, is like a power nap, as the humans call it. I need less time to sleep than others."

He glances between Juniper and me.

"She doesn't have that power. She has others that I don't have. That, I can guarantee. She's one of the most powerful Witch Warriors we have. She can not only cast, but she's also skilled in hand to hand combat. She didn't even break a sweat earlier."

His gaze lingers on Juniper again. Something flashes in his eyes, echoing the fire we sit beside. Why is he there protect her?

"Did someone hire you to protect her?" I ask.

His eyes widen. "No, I haven't been hired by anyone."

I want to know more about him. Juniper's an adult, but that doesn't make me less protective of her. She's more than my mentee. She is the daughter I never had.

"Why are you here?" I ask.

"Did you decide to stay awake with me so you could interrogate me? I'm not here to cause any kind of trouble. Yet I'm here for her. This is the truth. We shouldn't be debating this now. You completed your mission. Why are you still here? I know for a fact that when a Witch Warrior fulfills her duty, she needs to go back to the coven so that she can surrender the rescued magical object." He meets my gaze without flinching.

"You're right," she says. "But since I'm her mentor, I have a different purpose. That means that I will stay with her until she completes her mission."

Drake drops more twigs on the fire. After he finishes, the silence falls heavy upon us.

"You should go to sleep," I finally tell him.

"I don't need to sleep the same way most of you do."

I look at him, trying to think of any shifters that don't need sleep.

"Stop looking at me like that. I'm not the enemy here." His eyes shift. They look more reptilian than anything else.

I jab my thumb toward sleeping Juniper. "Why do you want her to know first?"

He takes up a stick and continues playing in the fire, as though he's determined to keep the flame alive and needs silence to do it. I'm sure he's hiding something big, so I squint at him, letting my energy guide my gaze, and his aura becomes clear to me. It seems to be the same kind of aura the Elders have: powerful and ancient.

"I can tell you're very old, way older than you pretend to be. It shows in your magic energy and in your aura, too."

"I'm not avoiding your question. I simply don't want to answer it. I could lie, but I know that you will catch the change in my aura if I do."

He's right about that.

Not all creatures can read that kind of information inside of magic energy and aura, but witches can. Some have specialized in that field. Usually, they keep them at the headquarters to serve in the interrogation rooms because they can tell truth from lies easily.

I smile. "You know a lot about us, but we don't know much about you."

"You and Juniper will never leave well enough alone, will you? You're right. I'm old. I stopped counting three centuries ago. Even then, I was old."

Satisfied with his admission, I stretch without much relief. Sleeping outside like this is hard on my muscles and joints.

"What can you tell me about her?" he dares to ask.

"Well, you know that she's a Witch Warrior. One of the best. There's more, but you will need to discover it yourself, or ask her – but if you do, be prepared to answer some questions about yourself, too. Juniper is very curious about nature and tenacious at gaining information. You know most of us spend our lives studying and specializing in our arts. We all have jobs that are assigned according to our power. For her age, Juniper always gets the hardest jobs. They always turn into a suicide mission at some point. The top Witch Warriors of Juniper's kind are way older than she is, and some witches want Juniper out of the coven because they consider her a freak, but she doesn't care. She's devoted to her missions."

"So, you only plan to tell me what I know or suspect. But why is she a freak to some?"

I get up to my feet and stretch again. "That's something

she will need to tell you. I will not say anything else. The same way you keep secrets from us. That's only fair. You can question her, but we got a faerie with us. Don't ask right now."

He gets up as well – he's tall enough to tower over me, even though my height is nothing to scoff at. "Maybe it's because she's the first one I've ever met. I know a lot about Witch Warriors, and your faction in general. But I can tell there's more than what she's shown me. That's the part that intrigues me."

The stars twinkle overhead. The night outside must be gorgeous. The only thing missing is a little breeze from outside.

"You will have to open yourself to us if you want her to open herself to you. If you continue like this, she will move on. Though, I suspect you want to keep her off-balance."

He chuckles. "It's late. I still need some sleep before the sun comes up."

Without asking anything else, I leave him to his guard duty. I sit, put my back against one of the trees close to the fire, then crook my finger.

"*Stratum.*"

A magical blanket appears around me, warming me. The night is not that cold, but having a blanket helps me fall asleep. I let myself go into the darkness and hope that I will not dream about my mate. The nightmares have been getting stronger than before.

I know the veil between the realm of the living and the dead grows thin. But there's something else... like my mate is closer than I believe. I feel him nearby as though I can touch him, but I wonder why he never comes when Juniper summons him.

What message does he have for me?

I let my thoughts slip from my grasp. I need my sleep, too, because tomorrow we still need to find the missing stone relic.

Our enemies will not waste any time. They will try to surround us as soon as they wake.

CHAPTER TWELVE

JUNIPER

I WAKE UP FEELING LIKE I HAVE A HANGOVER. I SCRUB MY hand over my face and then scan the surroundings.

"Good morning." Drake's voice sends the sleep away almost instantly.

I spin toward him and scowl. "What are you doing here?"

He's lying beside me, like we're a cozy couple. "You had a very busy night. When I got close, you crashed. So, I made the decision to stay with you all night." He grins at me.

I want to wipe the smirk off his face. "I'm awake, and I'm fine, so you can go back to your place." His face gets closer and I freeze. I never froze before in my life.

"My place is with you, even if you don't know yet," he says, "or do I need to remind you of that by kissing you again?"

I push him out of my way and stand up, wanting to hit him, hurt him. Yet, at the same time, I want to pull him into my lap, want to feel him as close as he can get. I shake my head. I need to get my mind back into the zone right now. It would be too easy to get lost in him.

My mission isn't finished. Until it's completed, I will have to keep my desires to myself. I glance at Lilandra and Marie. They're stirring, probably woken by our talking. Lilandra smiles at me. I wonder what he said to her about me, but then I pinch myself. The mission is the priority; the rest is not.

Marie looks around. "I will see if we can find some fruit and fresh water here."

I nod. "Be careful. We don't know if there are other traps, or even if the fruit and water are safe to consume."

"Don't worry, Lilandra. We fae know if any item is magical or rotten. That's part of our skills. We are in tune with the nature of objects."

Lilandra crosses her arms. "That may be so, but don't forget this is not a regular forest. This one comes with a very powerful kind of magic. Some things might be hidden from your knowledge here."

Marie nods and leaves.

"You're sure it's fine to let her go alone?" I ask Lilandra, drawing closer to her.

Lilandra glances at me. "Maybe, or maybe not. We don't know, but what choice do we have right now?"

I sigh. "None."

Lilandra puts a hand on my shoulder. "So, then, it's time to trust your gut. Mine tells me she's reliable, and that we can trust her."

"I trust you," I grin, "and your gut, so that means I will trust her. Did you have a good discussion with Drake last night?" I didn't want to sound too eager to know.

Lilandra smiles at me, glancing at Drake. "Yes and no. If you're wondering if he told me what he is, he didn't. He said that you'll be the first to know."

I study Drake. He's across the clearing, busy starting a fire from nothing. "He is old. He plays with fire like a wizard, but he isn't one. No shifter I've seen or read about can do things like that. " I turn to Lilandra. Something is changing in her aura, but it's like nothing I've seen before. "You seem at peace?"

Lilandra raises her gaze to mine. "Possibly. Decades of searching for it, but I didn't receive any call from it until now." She looks at the ring. "What does the ring do?" She gives it to me. There's a crow etched into it.

"That ring belonged to Robert the Bruce. It's linked to the Stone of Destiny. I suspect that's the stone that you need to save."

I nod. "Yes, that's the stone. Celestia told me where it was. She was able to get some information for me, but not much. One thing is right. The place where it's hidden is not natural." Long strands of hair fall over my forehead. It's a mess from a night sleeping on the ground, so I run my fingers through it, trying to put it back into braids.

Lilandra grabs my hand and looks at the ring I'm wearing. "What's this?"

"I DON'T KNOW. I got it from Celestia — she said that it belongs to me because, apparently, it holds a part of my energy."

Lilandra's eyes widen and she turns to stare at Drake.

I scowl at her. "What's going on?" She's clearly discovered something.

"It's nothing."

"Doesn't look like nothing."

Lilnadra's mouth puckers. Finally, she says, "There's a dragon crest on that ring. I thought they were extinct centuries ago."

I shrug. "I don't know anything about that. I've never studied them."

"If Celestia gave it to you, it's because it belongs to you. That little girl would never give you something to hurt you."

I touch the ring. "True, except she's not a little girl, but more like a teenager." I smile at Lilandra.

"Well, for me every female that's younger than me is a little girl, and that applies to you, too."

I glare. "No way. I'm twenty-five; I'm not a little girl. Take that back." I jump on her and start to tickle her.

"I won't take it back. Look out!" She uses magic to push me off her.

"Oh, no, you don't!"

"Stop it. Both of you," Marie yells at us.

I start to laugh and Lilandra does, too.

"This is childish," Marie says, marching toward us. "Here, have the fruit and water. They're safe to consume. I didn't see anything that could hurt us." She's placed everything on a large leaf, and she puts it on the ground between us.

"Marie is right. I can smell nothing on them, except that they are good for us," Drake adds when he joins us.

No one takes anything. Suspicion is too strong.

"Okay. I'll go first." Marie takes one of the pieces of fruit and then a sip of water. "There. Are you satisfied? None of it is poisonous."

I can't stop smiling while I grab a fruit. I have no idea what it's called, but the purple colors are bright and vibrant. When I put it in my mouth, it tastes like mango.

Lilandra picks up another one and so does Drake. We feast on the fruit, but then I notice a strange effect: the fleshy sweetness stirs my magic, and it rises in a frenzy.

A jolt hits me. In a flash, I understand the path to the stone is right in front of us, and that it's the same path Donovan and his group will be taking.

I expected this to be an easy task.

I'm mistaken yet again.

I glance at Drake. What other things could I be wrong about, too?

DONOVAN

"Hey, love. Wake up." My mate's voice whispers in my ear. Without opening my eyes, I smile. She loves waking me up.

"I'm awake," I say. When I open my eyes, my beautiful mate is looking down at me.

"You're all healed," she says. "We need to move. I made some breakfast. Everything here is edible. Thankfully."

I sit up. The rest of the group is gathering around a fire that Sophia provided. The food smells divine. I take some fruit, although my wolf and I would both prefer meat.

Lucas hands me a strip of something. "Meat," he says. "I come prepared."

"Thanks, friend. It'll be useful." I need my beef, but a big, juicy steak will have to wait. We need the stone. Once done, we'll also need to get that damn ring back.

The demon doesn't eat anything.

"You don't eat?"

He turns to us. "No. I can't find what I eat around here. I'm like the vampire when it comes to that, but I'm good for a few weeks. Hopefully, the mission will be finished by the time I need to feed again."

I turn to the vampire. "Jeremy?"

"I'm fine. Being a mature pure blood helps. I will need blood in about a week, so we have some time to work with. If we're not finished by then, I will have to do something."

I nod, understanding. Their needs are very different from

ours.

"If everyone is ready, we've got to move. That stone is close. The ring showed me its location just before it was taken, and there's a scent of it in the air that I can track."

Sophia stops beside me and grabs my hand, squeezing hard. "We will find both."

I take a deep breath. I wish I had her faith in all this. I want to know more about what the Lady is pushing us toward. We have a little army at our disposal. If we told everyone what we want to achieve, I'm certain that more would join us.

Why all this secrecy? Why not talk to everyone in the neutral zone? I'm certain others are in the same situation that we are right now.

"Love?"

I glance at my mate. "Yes?"

"You were far away. What's bothering you?"

"Just some thought. I wonder if we're doing the right thing in all this."

"For the stone, you mean?"

I kiss her cheek. "No, the whole operation, from day one."

She takes my hand. "Then what do you mean? We've been on mission after mission, non-stop for a couple of months."

"I just wonder if the Lady's strategy is the best one. We could be more straightforward. We can't be the only ones who want the boundaries to fall."

"I know, love, but we were supposed to be undercover for a long time. Damaris is the one responsible for that. Not the Lady. She did her best. But because of Damaris, the Vampire Internal Affairs *and* the Supernatural Intelligence Agency are both on the case. Other internal affairs from other factions have also joined the investigation. That doesn't help anything."

I smile at her. "You're right." Then I kiss her.

"We need to move, alpha. In which direction?" Lucas asks.

I take a deep breath. The smell of that stone is implanted in my brain. "The scent is stronger down that path. Watch out for the enemy, though. We are not alone."

As a group, we take the right path in the forest. The sun is up and bright. I look at Jeremy with concern, but nothing shows that he will burn and turn in ashes.

"What?" Jeremy asks.

"Nothing, I'm just concerned about the sun."

"Don't worry, my friend. It's not the sun, but only a reflection of it. The ultraviolet light is not in the beams, so it doesn't injure me." He raises his chin toward the light. "I've never been in the light like this. I'm beginning to understand why humans love it so much." He continues on his way.

My mate looks at me, her face wreathed in smiles.

We all know this is the calm before the chaos. We are not alone in this place. We are not the only ones hunting for the stone, and we know that they know, too. No surprise for anybody.

The forest is deep and filled with big trees. Each one might be centuries old. Grass covers the ground. This is a kind of forest that I would live in, if I could.

Trees like this don't grow in or around Montreal. Lucky that we have a big piece of land in the Laurentide. It provides a sense of freedom during the full moons. Each of the different packs in town own land like this.

We all need to have a place to run and refresh ourselves before returning to the concrete and asphalt jungle of the big city. Most factions prefer private places. We can use the streets to travel together, but we can't intermingle with other species. This is forbidden.

This is why I fight this war. I fight for the future. These

missions are vital to our success. My mate is not part of any pack, but she is from a different magical species than I am. This hope of freedom has become my lifeline. I need to be with my mate *and* my pack. We need to succeed so that others like us can find their fated mate.

"Love, we will succeed," she says. "I can feel it in my magic energy. I trust you and the strength of our love."

I smile at her. It's a blessing to have her – without her, my life would be without love. We continue to walk until we come to a stop in front of a temple.

The stone is inside.

"It's in there?" Lucas asks.

"Yes, but my inner wolf warns me that it's full of traps. We need to be on guard." I scan the surroundings. I hope that we are the first one to arrive at this temple. If we are, it may give us time to find it and be out of this place.

~

THE LADY

My assistant just entered my office. I'm still peering out the window, planning for my triumph. "Do we have news, Selena?"

"No, but the other team should soon join forces with the first. Only time will tell."

I turn around and look at her. My office is always shrouded in darkness. I stay in the shadow, keeping my face hidden from the others. If they knew what I was, it would make everyone suspicious of me. If anyone must see me, I cast a spell to create an illusion of myself, but I keep who I am hidden.

"Have they arrived?"

"Yes, from what I can tell, they did find the same

entrance, and they are going toward the first team. We don't know yet when they will join them. As you wished, they remain radio silent, so we can only wait and see."

Selena spoke the truth. There was nothing more I could do. Everything is on Donovan's shoulders, as the one in charge. He was the first one I convinced to join my mission. He is a good follower, but he has his mate, which allowed me to deceive him, to make it seem like we have the same goals. He wishes for freedom to live in the open as fated mates, and he doesn't know my real reasons for any of the missions I send him on.

"Do you think it will be impossible for them to succeed?"

I turn back to Selena. She's another follower that believes everything I've said. Her trust in me is complete.

"They will," I say. "You know that Donovan has too much to lose if he fails. The mission is crucial for him, which will push him to do everything in his power to succeed."

Selena nods and then leaves me to myself. It should be daylight for Donovan's team. Here, it's night time. I need less sleep than I used to, as my thoughts are consumed by my desire for revenge. All of them will pay for the fact they exiled me to another realm and turned my beautiful body into that of a crippled old woman.

But I don't want to go there tonight. Those emotions serve their purpose: to help me in my only mission. I don't care about the factions. I will make them suffer too. Chaos is my new friend, and I will push everyone to the edge of insanity. I want everyone to believe that anyone could be their enemy, even someone in their own family.

Yes, everyone will pay. My revenge will be brutal and merciless.

I will be the master of the beautiful chaos, and all of humankind will have to pledge themselves to me.

I will become the queen of everything.

CHAPTER THIRTEEN

JUNIPER

"Do you think we are the first to find it?" Marie asks me.

I study the temple in front of us. It seems off somehow. The stone is inside, deep below the surface. "Yes, it's still there. The pull is still very strong, but the stone is underneath the temple. We need to enter in order to follow the path that will take us where we need to go."

Marie nods.

"The ring tells me the same thing, too. We are on the right path. I'm glad we have its help, since it's linked to the stone, and they need each other."

I glance at Lilandra. I don't feel anything from the ring she retrieved from Donovan. "Do you think they are still healing from the fight?"

"This, I can answer," Drake offers. "They were recently here, and they want us to believe we're alone, but I can smell them. I'm sure they are around."

I turn to him. He's standing beside me, but I don't want

to think or feel anything. I can't let myself think about him yet. My focus is on that stone. That's my first priority.

"So, what's next? If they're here already, how will we pull this off?" Marie asks.

As one, we all turn to face the building in front of us. There are several flights of stairs to climb before we can enter the temple. I try to check the aura that surrounds us, but I get nothing from it. The place has too much magic energy that makes my readings confusing, so I can't rely on that.

"What do you think, Juniper? You're the one with the pull. The stone is talking to you. You have the chance to see other things. Anything there?" Lilandra asks me.

The three of them look at me. Geez. *Thank you, Lilandra.* She put me on the spot. Witch Warriors usually work alone. We have secrets to keep. Though, in my case, it's more than that. Lilandra knows it, but the others don't.

"No, nothing. Only the pull from the stone and the message to come save it. That's the only thing I have. Too much magical energy here to be able to see anything else." I focus on Lilandra as I speak.

I want her to understand I can't see or feel dead people here, but nobody else needs to know that. They probably suspect something, so I can't afford to be any clearer with Lilandra at this time.

My mother's secret gift belongs to me alone. I haven't even told anyone in the coven about it, and the only reason Lilandra knows is by mistake. I used it once, when we needed it. One thing that my mother told me before she died is that nobody, whether human or any paranormal species, understands the gift of being a medium.

Lilandra nods.

"Well, I guess the only thing we can do is to go inside," Marie tells us.

We start up the stairs and reach the entrance. On the

outside, it resembles old Incan temples, or something built by an equally old civilization, yet the wooden door entrance seems brand new. The mission is mine, so I take the lead.

Usually, my arrival can neutralize some of the traps set to protect the magical object, because I answer the call to rescue it, not steal it. But maybe the other team tripped a few of the traps before we arrived. I take a breath. Here we go.

"Anyone need light?" I ask.

All of them nod. Lilandra and I cast spells to help us see. I know fairies can see in the dark, and, from experience, I know that Drake can, too.

We enter the darkened hallway. Long ago, the majestic corridor would have been lit by magic, impressive to any and all that came here.

"Why did they build this?" Marie asks.

"This place is very old – maybe it wasn't built with the intention of housing the stone. Perhaps not even the old books hold the answer to that mystery," Lilandra answers.

I get another pull. "The stone is to the left. Do you smell anything, Drake? You said we weren't alone, but are they on the same path as us?"

Drake stops and closes his eyes. For a moment it feels as though I can breathe through his nose. He takes a deep breath. "They are – might be up to an hour ahead of us. Do you think they already have the stone?" he asks me.

"No. Usually, if that happens, the call becomes more frenzied and the pull repeats frantically. That's not happening, so I don't think they have it. They may be close to the stone but still looking for it."

I move toward my pull once more. "Lilandra, is it always like this for Witch Warriors?"

"Yes, Juniper, it's something we can't control," she answers.

"What happens when you are too old to go on missions?"

"Normally, others are available to take the call. The magical object always calls the best one for them. I'm a jewel specialist, and Juniper is a stone specialist. There are a lot of Witch Warriors, but only a few in each of different specialities. In her case, Juniper is the only stone specialist. In mine, I'm one of two jewel specialists. However, the ring called me instead of the other one because of the past history I have with it. When Witch Warriors get too old, others come to take our place, and they become the champion the relics call. But some stay in the field even though they are old, because they are still the best there is. Not all of the Witch Warriors are in best shape, but usually they are."

Marie looks at me and then Lilandra. "Thank you for the information. I wasn't sure how this all works."

We continue on in silence, trying to stay as quiet as we can.

I stop the group. I didn't think it would matter, but it must be the day before Halloween. "Fuck!" I yell.

"What is it?" Marie asks.

I don't answer. I don't want to.

"What is it, Juniper?" Lilandra tries to catch my attention.

No, not now. Necromancy is a gift.

I meet her gaze and I try to speak, but nothing happens. My whole body trembles. The next twenty-four hours are going to be the worst I've ever experienced. I've figured out what the temple is.

It's not just a temple. It's a tomb.

We're right in the middle of a war cemetery.

∾

DONOVAN

"Are we still alone?" I ask the demon.

"No, they are right behind us, and catching up," he says, looking over his shoulder.

I look at my mate and then at my beta. "We need to move. I might not have the ring anymore, but I can still trace the energy that shows me the way. My wolf wants to be out of this place. It's getting creepier than ever."

Sophia studies me. "Love, the magic here is so much stronger than outside. I don't know what the purpose of this temple was, but magic permeates every stone. I don't understand why there weren't any traps yet. We should have come across many."

I didn't think too much about all this. That question came to my mind but I refused to answer it or spend time worrying about it. It's almost like someone wants us to find the stone. I frown. Or maybe a bigger trap is waiting for us.

"This place would have been beautiful in the past. But I'm still trying to figure out why it's here?" Sophia stares at the ceiling. It's true that, at one point, the temple would have been gorgeous. Maybe not everything was in the forest when it was built; maybe it used to be a garden.

I turn around. "Jeremy, you're the oldest here. Do you know of any places like this?"

"I'm not sure. It might have been here for a long time, but I never heard about it. Vampires keep to themselves more. Sophia, you witches record the history of the entire paranormal community – have you ever heard about something like this?"

Sophia frowns. "No, I wasn't a scholar. The Librarian is the only one that might know. It's her job to study magic, which is the reason why all the magical objects rescued by the Witch Warriors are brought to her. She is the foremost scholar and chronicler of the paranormal community, the only one that knows everything about anything magic related – not only objects, creatures, or species, but any kind of history."

"How do we reach the Librarian?" the demon asks.

"From what I know, the Librarian's successor just arrived. She is very young, but powerful, since the old Librarian gave her his knowledge in a prestigious ceremony. That's how all information that's ever been found is kept from Librarian to Librarian. Before I decided to leave my coven to be with my mate, the new Librarian turned reckless. She didn't like the fact she was the chosen one."

"That means you don't know anything more than any of us?"

Sophia shrugs. "No. Maybe Jeremy knows some stories, but I wouldn't be able to tell if it's only a myth or the truth. My training was only to learn to control my fire inside and be a caster. I'm the strongest in the fire element, but I know nothing of the histories. We train according to our strengths and everyone keeps to their own section of the larger whole. That's why the coven is strong in the faction. We each have our own job."

"Jeremy?"

He looks at me. "I only know one fairy tale, a story that is told to children, passed down from generation to generation. But whether it's accurate, I couldn't say."

"Tell us anyway," I request.

We gather around him. "Demon, how much time do we have?"

He looks back. "At best, maybe an hour."

I nod to Jeremy. "How long will your story take?"

"I'll finish it in ten minutes," Jeremy says.

I nod at him. "Once it's finished, we still have a mission to do."

We continue walking, but slower, so the sounds of our footsteps don't drown out Jeremy's story.

"One of my father's stories went like this. Long ago, a group of strong magic users, maybe wizards, witches, warlocks, or others, came here to create an underground city. That was centuries ago. I don't know if this is accurate, but for many centuries, paranormal explorers searched for this city. They wanted the gold, ancient spells, or the manuscripts that were lost — maybe some forbidden magic that is now lost to time."

"To me, this resembles the human tales about Conquistadors who searched for the Incan temples of gold. So many searched, but most of them died and never returned. Nobody knew if it existed or where to look, but the description that has been gathered from old texts is very similar to this. Again, that could be something else entirely. However, they always went searching for ancient magic, scrolls, or manuscripts to be able to learn from arts that are not known anymore. The vampire community tried a couple of times but never succeeded: many vampire explorers died or disappeared without a trace. The ones that managed to come back said that it was deadly beautiful, but too powerful for anyone to discover its secrets."

"Why have the werewolves never heard about this?" I ask aloud.

"Maybe the stories of the temple came before your kind, before Lillith had committed her crime that created the werewolves."

We continue down the corridor, getting closer to the stone. My skin prickles, and my wolf wants to claw his way out, snarling and jumping inside of me.

"Over the years, we've started telling this story as a cautionary tale that teaches us how blindly seeking something is not always good, even for immortal vampires like us. I always believed this was a lesson for us. It's important to understand that shiny things may not be a good thing, even if we want them."

After the story, I'm quiet. We know from human history how sought after these lost cities were. Could the Incas have been a magical kingdom, too? Us finding something so very much like Incan ruins here, in the middle of nowhere, might be a clue pointing in that direction. Nobody lived here or continued to thrive in this place.

We press on toward the stone. We need it. The questions can be answered afterward. The mission is the priority. How could this place still be so full of magic?

It's like someone is still here.

But who could it be, and how can they still be alive?

∼

MARIE

I glance around. In another time, long ago, this place would have been most beautiful.

I study my little group. I'm part of the faeries' internal affairs agency. They asked me to investigate what the Supernatural Intelligence Agency and other internal affairs in the different factions were up to. It's good to know what others are working on.

Whatever is going on is bigger than any of us. I'll have no choice but to tell my superior what I discovered. Someone is trying to reverse the rules of the factions and the government.

I turn to Lilandra. "Do you think this was done for a reason?"

Lilandra may be a Witch Warrior, but she's more than fair. Us faeries don't mingle with other species a lot. We rather stay behind the scenes. Unfortunately, some members of the faction have been disappearing. We know they are alive. We have a life specialist in our faction that can trace anyone, but it's like they didn't want to be discovered.

"Maybe, but why are the faeries' internal affairs interested in all this? I know that you are more separatist than others have been with different species."

I consider all of them. Lilandra is more like a maternal figure. She's hot-headed when it comes to Juniper, but her overall disposition is calm. I don't know all of her history. One thing I do know is that she lost her mate during one of her missions. By the way Juniper tells it, this ring was the cause of it.

"Some members of our community have gone missing. That's unusual for us."

"So, that's why you are following Lilandra around?" Juniper asks.

"Yes. I know that Witch Warriors go where they are called. We suspected that, since so many of you were on missions these last few months, that it must be related somehow."

That's all the information that I can give right now. I'm sad for Lilandra, though. If it was just her asking, maybe I might be inclined to tell more.

"You're spying on us?" Juniper asks, sneering at me.

"No, we are trying to understand," I tell Juniper. She's really pissing me off right now.

"Stop it, Juniper. Everyone is on edge right now. Too much is going on for it not to be related. You can come to us with questions and concern. I know the SIA wants all of us to work together on this. Some have more information, but combining it all will help all of us."

Lilandra is trying to calm down the situation, but I stand

by my point. I'm still pissed at Juniper. I will see after that mission if my hunch is correct.

"Well, it's difficult to be honest when people are hiding things, and we are the ones that are doing the mission," Juniper complains.

She may be right, but now is not the time to cause problems. "Well, I've said what I can. The rest needs to wait. Besides, your mission is the priority one, is it not?"

Juniper shoots me a glare that reveals she has no control over her emotions at all – yet I'm sensing something else in her, too. The closer we get to Halloween, the more unstable she's becoming.

I need to figure out why.

CHAPTER FOURTEEN

JUNIPER

IF I WAS PISSED BEFORE, NOW I'M MAD.

That Marie faerie bitch just admitted she's spying on us. I close my eyes and take several breaths so I can calm down. Things are getting weirder the deeper into the temple-cave we go.

"Juniper?"

I open my eyes. "Yes?"

"For the sake of the mission, we need to get to the stone and fast. If what Drake said is true, that means they are ahead of us." Lilandra said.

I stroll deeper into the temple. Drake follows me but doesn't speak. Relieved, we leave the war cemetery behind. It'll be much better for me. I know a lot of ghosts are here, and the veil between our world and the hereafter is growing thinner. Soon, they'll start to cross between the realms.

"I know. And not only that – if my calculations are right, the eve of Halloween is in two days."

Lilandra frowns. "You've never been on a mission in that period."

I sigh. "Yes, true. Add to that that it's different than ever before, because everyone's on edge and there's a lot of magical energy already popping around. That's not good, Lilandra – it's like we are closing in on something big and evil. Do you know what I learned just before I came here?"

We climb the rest of the stairs. It's better for me to be far away from the ground. At most, I still have two days before *that* night arrives. If I'm still here when it does, it will be my worst nightmare come true.

Luckly, Lilandra is with me, and she knows what will happen. The jolt from earlier is usually the first phase. It will be dangerous for me once Halloween comes. I have no choice when it comes to this.

"The faster we do this, the faster will be back with the coven. There, you will be able to pass Halloween without any problems. For now, you just need to be on your guard. For sure, being in this kind of place isn't helping you."

I look around the temple. We're on an upper level, and we have a better view looking down into the temple. Everything seems so peaceful and quiet, but I know better. I have enough experiences that have scarred me for life. There's nothing calm about the building we're in.

"I have no choice, and you know it. Listen, there's a situation that doesn't help any of us. It's not even public yet, and I hope that day never arrives." I lean closer to Lilandra and I start to whisper. "Zoe told me that the Paranormal University is under attack by a very old wizard seeking revenge on us."

Lilandra freezes. "Don't tell me the legend is true?"

"Apparently, it always has been. Some don't believe it but, from what Zoe told me, the university has been attacked, and the SIA: Special Operations Team is there to help them, but that's all I know. Some magic users were killed there."

"Fuck. We can't do anything for them. They have a whole team with them to help, but we do need to discover our relic quickly so we can offer our assistance too. So, what are we doing next?"

I can't say more than what's already been said, so I step through the dark entrance and cross my fingers that we'll be able to find that stone before the others.

The magical pull of the stone is so strong that it distracts me from the fact that the veil is growing thinner by the second.

~

DONOVAN

"The night is coming quickly," Jeremy tells me.

We've been inside the temple for hours and still haven't found the stone. The part of my skin that had the ring is tingling – some of the magic remained in my skin, allowing me to find our way through the temple. We are descending so deep that we should be experiencing some physical signs of pressure and lack of oxygen, but I guess the magic helps with that problem.

Some of our team has come from my pack, like Lucas, but the others are from other factions. I never dreamed I'd be a part of something like this in my lifetime. Five years ago, if someone had said that I would mate a witch and lead a rebellion, I would have called them crazy liars.

"You seem far away, my love."

We can be anywhere, and she will always be the most beautiful woman in the world to me. We have had days and nights without any sleep and not even a bed to lay on, and she never complained.

"I thought that if someone had told me five years ago who

I'd mate and who I'd become, I wouldn't have believed them," I say.

She giggles. "Yes, same here. A lot has happened, and more needs to happen still in order for us to be together all the time. We must shatter those faction barriers."

I stop.

"What is it?" she asks.

"The itching on my skin is getting stronger. I never thought embedding that ring could still help us to find that stone."

"Which way?" Jeremy asks.

I try to make my wolf to smell around and help me find that stone, without success.

Sophia says, "You can't smell magic like that. Your wolf may already smell it, but doesn't know it belongs to the stone."

I smile at her, and we resume walking down the stairs going down into infinity. "We need to continue down. None of these doors lead anywhere. What do you see, Demon?"

"Stairs," the demon answers.

"Ok, I'm fed up with these stairs," Sophia complains.

I give her a kiss on the lips. "I know. Me, too. But the stone is somewhere below us, I'm sure of it. Demon, try again. What do you see?"

"My eyesight is good, but I only see stairs. I think there's a light below, though. We need to continue, I think we'll find another chamber," he answers.

We continue going down. The demon is right. A chamber appears at the bottom and a light shows us a way and which corridor to follow. I hope that will be the end of our search, but we'll need to climb up the long staircase again after.

"Someone loves the fire element here. There's magic in the lights," Sophia tells us.

"You think that someone put the light here by magic? How long have those been here?" Lucas asks.

"By the smell, a very long time, but I could be wrong," I reply.

At the end of the corridor, there's a large door, only nine feet in front of us.

"It's sealed by magic. I wonder what can open it?" Grace says.

"Any ideas?" I ask the group.

"You think that ring could open it?"

I shake my head. "No, for some reason, that was only the beacon to get here. Demon, you want to try opening the door?"

The demon snarls at me and barrels through us. As he begins to push on the heavy door, it starts to open slowly. Inch by inch, he's able to crack the door open wide enough for us to enter into an enormous room.

In its center, perched upon a stand with a light shining down on it, is the stone we're looking for.

"Do you know where that light is coming from? Do you think it's fine to touch it?"

You never know when energy magic can be wrong. It could lead to deadly traps. Sophia approaches the stand and touches the ray of light.

I move to stop her, but she's too far from me. Fortunately, the light doesn't seem to hurt her. "You think it's safe?" I ask.

"Well, safe enough to touch it. Will something trigger when we touch the stone? That's another story, but we need to try anyway. I will do it, since I can attack with fire." She reaches for the stone.

I thought that the stone was way bigger than it actually is. That's lucky, since at the beginning I planned for the demon to carry it. We didn't need him for that, but if he hadn't come along, that door would have stayed shut. I'm strong but not like him.

I stay close to Sophia. Her fingers almost touch the stone. At first, she strokes it gently to test for traps, but nothing happens. She takes a deep breath and picks it up, resting it on her palm. The dark stone is transparent.

I can sense the magic inside it.

"That's much better." She smiles and shows it to us. "Here is the Stone of Destiny, the stone whose makes people follow the leaders they never would have followed otherwise."

I reach for the magical stone, but she pulls it back.

"No, love – I think it didn't do anything to me because I'm a witch, but I'm not sure what it would do to you."

I nod. She may be right. Now all we have to do is get out before Juniper and her group arrive.

"We need to move and get back to the headquarters as fast as possible. I want this place out of my sight."

We hurry out of the room and to the base of the staircase. The faster we go, the better I like it. Sophia and Grace cast a spell that lifts us up toward the main entrance of the temple. When I glance down, we're much closer to the light above, and it's very dark below.

We need to get gone.

≈

LILANDRA

It's so dark inside the temple.

I expected light. "Do you think it's normal to have no light inside? They should have a plan to have some. Juniper, are you still getting the pull?"

I glance at my mentee. I know it's hard for her right now. The veil between realms is getting thinner. With a pull like the one from the stone, things could get wild. Her magic will be stronger than usual.

"Something's not right," Juniper says. "The pull is coming closer to us, but we aren't moving. That's not good."

A gust of wind blows against us, as Donovan and his group whip past, leaving the temple... and they have the stone.

"Fuck!" she screams, and immediately casts the spell to run faster.

I follow her without stopping to say anything to Drake or Marie. Juniper is my priority right now. She takes her katana in one hand and her gun in the other and peppers Donovan's group with bullets. Luckily, nobody can see us.

"Give me that stone, it doesn't belong to you," she screeches and makes her spell faster. That's what I expect from her. She doesn't see danger when she's in this state.

Sophia laughs at her. "You, miss, do you have a problem with your focus?"

"Juniper, stop. We'll get them, but you need to clear your head and think," I yell at her.

She doesn't respond, only focusing on her mission.

I cast my gun spell to help Juniper stop them, but a witch in Donovan's group casts an earth wall. *Fuck*. Another burst of wind careens toward us. It's coming from behind and getting closer.

I shoot. Then I glance over my shoulder, and my jaw drops at I'm seeing: Drake is running like crazy, and he's got Marie on his back. No shifter I know has that kind of power.

"What are you doing, Drake?" I bellow.

"Now is not the time," he answers. "I have to reach her. What she's doing is too dangerous! Can you make space for Marie?"

I nod at him and create another running cloud which he puts Marie onto before he bursts forward, running faster.

He's trying to reach Juniper. I look to Marie. She has her sword at the ready.

She shrugs. "Don't ask me. He put me on his back and started running like crazy. We can discuss it later – now we've got a fight to win."

I concentrate on both the running cloud and my magic gun as we get closer.

All of a sudden, for a reason I don't understand, all of them are down, and Drake is beside Juniper. He grabs her arm and pushes her behind, protecting her with his body.

"Argenti!"

I don't want to kill Donovan. I know what it is to lose a mate. But I do want to put him out of commission and then take the stone away from them.

"If you think you can hit him again, Lilandra, you're wrong," Sophia calls.

Juniper doesn't know that Sophia was my best friend – though, based on Sophia's behavior, she doesn't think of me as one anymore. Sophia casts a flame spell at me, and I barely avoid taking the full force of it, but it still grazes me and makes me wince. I strain to keep my focus on her. She's the one that could make everything go wrong.

I shoot again as Donovan transforms himself into a werewolf so he can move faster. Drake is handling the demon. Lucky that we have him with us – he may be a mystery, but so far he's been extremely useful.

Juniper charges Donovan again. I suspect he's got the stone, but another werewolf stands beside him.

"Let go of that stone," Juniper warns them.

"Lilandra, tell your mentee to stop bugging us. You know I don't like her ever since you refused to give us the Seal of Solomon for her sake."

Juniper stops in her tracks and looks at me. "What the hell is she talking about?"

I sigh. "This is not the right place to talk about it. I promise that I will discuss it with you later. For now, focus." I want her focused on the mission, instead of overthinking everything like she usually does.

"No, not now, my best friend, my enemy. Tell her, or I will."

I concentrate on keeping my gun trained on Donovan as I summon another twelve guns to float in the air around me.

"Stop, Sophia. You're forgetting to protect something." One of my bullets lodges into Donovan's shoulder. I know I've only scratched him, but the shot will serve as a warning. "Next time, I will make more damage."

She rushes to her mate's side and then turns to stare at me. In the past, I could see trust and friendship in her face, but now there is only anger. Her magical aura is red like the flames she controls.

"Don't test me, Sophia," I say. "You know what I'm able to do."

She snarls at me. "Yeah, we all know. You decided: her over him. All you had to do was to give up the Seal, but, no, you chose otherwise."

"Fuck." Juniper peers around them. "The pull has shifted position."

The other werewolf and the earth witch rush toward the entrance. "It's them. There they are!"

Juniper charges them. "We got unfinished business, my friends."

I never wanted to have to face this situation. This is my nightmare.

Will I be able to kill Sophia in order to protect Juniper? She's so determined to stop me that I may not have any other choice. I don't want to separate fated mates, but killing both of them would solve that issue. That way I wouldn't have their separation on my conscience.

CHAPTER FIFTEEN

JUNIPER

"If you think you will get away with this, you're wrong," I scream at them.

They both turn around to glare at me.

"You don't know what you're dealing with," the werewolf says.

The witch conjures a spell, and the ground beneath us starts to move. Her skill is so different from a fire witch's. Chunks of earth lift up from the ground and sail toward me. I dodge the earth projectiles, darting all around them until one of them slams into me, throwing me to the ground.

A moment later, Drake is standing over me. "Miss me?" He grins. "Take care of the others. I will take care of him."

The earth witch distracted me so much I didn't notice the demon charging at me. I didn't see Drake attack the demon.

I roll my eyes at Drake. *That shifter*. All I want is to hit him as hard as I can. Instead, I take my weapons in each hand. It's nice to be ambidextrous.

"Argenti!"

My katana illuminates with the spell. The werewolf begins his shift into a wolf and the witch hurls more projectiles at me. A witch is not immune any time except when she is casting a spell.

The werewolf runs on all fours toward me – he'll be close enough to lunge in seconds. I draw my katana into a defensive position and stabilize my gun hand on top of it. I squeeze the trigger, but he dodges each of the bullets, thanks to the witch moving him up and down with her earth ability. As the ground shifts beneath me, it throws me off-balance, making it impossible to hit a shot.

My only option is the katana. If I get close, she'll make me and him move at the same time. That will give him an advantage, but she doesn't know what I'm capable of.

The werewolf bares his teeth and drool drips from his jaw. He means business, I'm sure of that. To the side, Drake still fights the demon. I smirk. No matter how I feel about him, it's lucky that we have Drake. Fighting that demon without Drake would be a real pain in the ass.

I turn to the werewolf. "Come on, if you want a piece of me."

Provoking a werewolf is not a good idea, but I'm out of options, and I need him to attack me. He has the stone, or maybe the witch does. If he runs at me, I can figure out who has it.

"I want that stone, you will give it to me. Now!" I yell.

I summon my magic and use it to fuel my attack. The spell enhances my fighting capability. The closer I get, the better I can tell that the pull comes from *her*, not from him, so I turn my attention to her. She continues to cast her spells to help him.

I flip around and drop to the ground. I have to find it. I charge her. "Give it to me."

She lifts a stone and hurls it at me. A piece of it hits me. I'm able to dodge most of it, it but—*fuck!*—that hurt.

"You cannot have it. It belongs to the Lady, and my mate needs it to complete his mission," she replies.

Now it makes sense. Not only is that werewolf her partner, he's her mate. That's why she protects him like this.

I gesture to her. "I'll let you both go if you give it to me. I promise."

She glances at the werewolf that's approaching from my left side, but she doesn't answer.

"I can kill both of you right now. But my mission is simple: I need that stone. You give it to me and you live." I never want to threaten any of my enemies, but sometimes I need to.

"No."

She continues to throw chunks of earth at me: each time, they get bigger. I suspect our opponents are heading toward a tunnel that will take them back to the surface. One of her big projectiles slams into me, and I lose my balance, stumbling over the floor until I fall. I shake my head, but it rocked me, and my vision blurs. I will have a big headache tomorrow, but I can't worry about that right now.

The pull drives me to continue. The stone screams for help.

Shit. I hate this. My brain is mush. I climb to my feet and look at them. I can see the stone. I can pinpoint it. It's in the left pocket of her jeans. I need to aim my magic there and make it fall on the ground. Surely, she will cast something to recover it, but, if it falls, it will give me plenty of time to make sure she doesn't pick it up.

I don't want to consider my mentor right now. I know she is able to take care of herself. Drake is, too. If they're all fine...

Where is Marie?

LILANDRA

"You're a fucking bitch, you know that, Lilandra?"

She's healing her mate. Both of them are back on their feet, and the vampire rejoined them, too. Well, I know that three against one is a challenge, but I can take them. I know Juniper pursues the one with the stone. I've got the ring embedded in my skin where it will stay.

"You're the bitch, Sophia. You're the one who keeps this fight going. You can leave and be with your mate, but both of you decided otherwise. The only possibility I see is that both of you will die today." I want to make them think of the consequences of what they are doing. I need to make Sophia understand. She will have a better life in the neutral zone. They don't need to sacrifice one or both of their lives.

"You don't understand. I thought you were the one that could understand everything, Lilandra. You lost him, not once, but twice now. And for what? So you could live your life like a shadow. Is your job better than having a life fulfilled by love? I pity you, who spit on the chance to have your mate back. You turned your back on me and rejected us all. Now you will pay for what you did to us. Give me back that ring, Lilandra. This is your last warning."

I grind my teeth as she glares at me. My magic energy is not a hundred percent yet, but that's fine. I've dealt with far worse situations in my life. "So be it, Sophia. We will see who is left standing on this day."

It's the end of the line for our friendship. No more can be said or done. We are too different from each other. If I kill her, I will kill them both. Neither of them will have to go through losing their mate.

No one will suffer as I did.

Donovan transforms into his werewolf and puts himself between me and her. The vampire is beside them. Donovan's claws and fangs are ready. She begins casting, but I know all her moves and her spells. We studied together at the Paranormal University and in the community as well.

Flames gather around them, turning to a shield. I conjure my machine gun and fill it with ultraviolet and silver bullets, glancing around to see if I can use the environment to my advantage. The way I see it, I will have to rely on my magic only. So, I grab my weapon, and I squeeze the trigger. They all start to move, dodging bullets. Sophia uses her fire to protect herself. I cast a magic shield around myself. I'll have to change to something else when we move to close combat.

Donovan reaches me first. The vampire guy, Jeremy, lags behind. Donovan growls at me and bares all his teeth before he launches himself at me, but I dodge him. His claws scratch long grooves in my magic shield. A moment later, the marks disappear. Thankfully, nothing serious.

"You're going down," Jeremy yells at me. He runs at me, so I change my machine gun for an assault rifle, still with silver and ultraviolet bullets, and use my shield for protection as I shoot him.

Jeremy laughs until the first bullet grazes him, but then he snarls. The ultraviolet bullets aren't lethal, but they will hurt him and slow him down, because he has to stop and heal.

I need to make time for Juniper to gather the stone so we can leave. The way I see it, I'm the distraction while Juniper fights for the stone and Drake takes the demon.

As Donovan charges me again, Sophia throws a fireball at me, so I double my efforts to slow Jeremy down by switching to a fully ultraviolet automatic and spraying him with bullets. It's a risky move, since I need different bullets for Donovan, but I have no choice.

"You will fail, Lilandra. Leave the ring and go."

"In your dreams, Sophia. I'm in it to the bitter end."

It'll be the last thing I say to her. She knows where I stand now. It won't be over until someone winds up dead.

She digs into the earth, making molten lava sip through to the surface. I know she wants to make me unstable, but I'm prepared for this.

More of my ultraviolet bullet hit Jeremy. The vampire is starting to slow down. Donovan attacks me, jumping on me, and I have no time to change the bullets back to silver so I can shoot him.

His claws pass through my shield this time, and he lands on my left shoulder. Pain shoots through me, but I'm fine. I cast a patch spell to stop the bleeding.

Now I focus on him. Through him, I will hit Sophia.

I conjure magic knives to throw at them. I need to make her stop casting spells, and I need to put her mate out of commission.

But something in the back of my head makes me realize I've missed something.

Where is Marie?

～

DRAKE

"You ever give up, shifter?" the demon growls.

I give him my cockiest smile. "Never. This is too much fun."

He snarls at me. "Fun?"

"Yes!" I punch him over and over, and he lands a few direct hits, too. My mate is fighting the werewolf and the witch. So far, everything is fine for her. Well, I hope it stays that way.

The demon slugs me in the face. With a crack, the impact

dislocates my jaw. He starts to laugh, but I snap my jaw back in place in one swift movement. "Well, now you're talking." A demon is strong, but an old dragon shifter is stronger.

"What are you, shifter?"

"You will never know. Maybe before you die, I will tell you."

Maybe or maybe not. The secret belongs to my mate, and she will know first. He continues to punch me, but I can tell, in his head, he really wonders what I am and how to kill me. There's a lot of things these creatures don't understand.

From the corner of my eye, I catch a glimpse of my mate. She's sexy when she's pissed. I could watch her fight like this all the time. But, first, I have to put the demon down. My mate is good, but I can't afford to lose her. If she dies, I'll be as good as dead, too. The demon comes at me again, and I shift my hand into a dragon claw.

The demon's eyes widen. "You're a..."

Before he can say anything else, I slash him to death with a single blow. He hits the ground as the life drains from him.

I turn and head back to my mate. The witch has nasty skills – she's able to change the structure of the ground.

The werewolf jumps at my mate, and I punch him, throwing him onto his back.

The witch stops casting and rushes toward him. "My mate!" she screams.

Oh, I didn't know. Juniper moves faster, and I can tell she's cast a run-fast spell on herself.

"Not so fast," Juniper tells the witch, grabbing at her jeans and ripping the left pocket open. The stone falls to the ground.

Juniper pushes the witch aside, but the witch continues toward her mate.

Juniper glances at the stone. It's faded brown, but starts to glow when Juniper touches it. She smiles at me. "We've got it. We can go." She turns around and looks at her mentor.

The fire witch screams at Lilandra. "You spit on the gift you were offered. You could have had him back, but you decided to stay with Juniper."

Juniper stops, apparently intrigued by what the witch is saying to her mentor.

"Lilandra, I got it," she calls. "Let's get out of here."

Lilandra nods and a host of different kinds of weapons appear at her back. Each one fires at her enemies. She uses the same run-fast spell. I have to run faster without revealing my secret to all of them.

"This tunnel seems to be leading outside. We will be out in no time."

We continue our flight. We have the stone, and we have the ring. The mission is a success, and we need to get back as soon as we can.

"Juniper, where's Marie?" I ask.

"I don't know and I don't care. She left us, so let her be. She can find her own way back. There's got to be more than one entrance in and out of here."

Why did the faerie decide to leave us now? We've succeeded, haven't we?

Then I hear something that brings me to a halt. That's when I yell. "Stop!"

CHAPTER SIXTEEN

JUNIPER

WE'RE IN THE TUNNEL. THE EXIT ISN'T FAR, BUT THAT'S when I see them.

Those bastards were bringing more allies with them. We are cornered – or it's more like we're sandwiched inside.

"We're not alone," Drake tells me.

I could conjure the running spell, but with all the fighting and the casting, my breath is short. I glance at Lilandra. She's worse off than me.

"WHY ARE WE STOPPING?" Lilandra whispers, taking a deep breath.

" They brought more backup, and we are stuck here between the two sides. We will have to fight them both." I scan the tunnel, searching for another way to escape, but we are stuck in the middle, in a place where the tunnel widens, which I suspect was a way to bring supplies and other goods in so that they can be redistributed inside.

"Lilandra, what did that witch say about me?"

She avoids looking at me. "Nothing."

I know when someone is lying or hiding something. "I can read your aura and tell that you're lying, you know."

"It doesn't concern you, and now it's not the time," Lilandra says.

" I want to know. Quick." I push Lilandra to tell me.

"You think this is the place or the time for it?" Drake interjects.

I ignore him. This is between me and Lilandra. "Now, Lilandra, I have a question." I pause. "Are you betraying us?"

I'm tall, but Lilandra matches my height, and we're eye to eye.

Lilandra glares at me, crosses her arms, and stomps her foot. "You think that I would betray the coven or the faction? You know me better than that – we have been together for almost a decade now. You're the reason why I didn't kill myself after my mate's death. You and all my other mentees make my life worth living."

She muttered something under her breath. "You don't know what you're talking about. I was young before, and I didn't hide how my mate got killed. Sophia, that fire witch, was my best friend during my time at Paranormal University and the coven. She's the one who dragged me out to party one night. That's where I met him."

"Best friend?"

Lilandra takes a deep breath and stares at me. Hurt, loneliness, and passion fill her gaze, but mostly, the emptiness of her heart shows through. "It's a past life, Juniper. She proposed something that I had to refuse."

Drake comes up behind me. "What was it?"

The magic torches following us are getting closer. Once they reach us, the spells in the light will expose our hiding places.

Lilandra doesn't speak, instead staring into middle distance.

"Tell me, Lilandra." I push her. I need to know. What kind of bargain did they offer her? Is that why Sophia got mad at me?

Lilandra winces and sighs. "She offered to resurrect my mate if I gave them the Seal of Solomon."

My mouth falls open. "No, that's impossible. They can't bring dead people back. It's been more than a decade and nobody with a bonded mate has been able to do it. That's unthinkable."

She places her hand on my shoulder. "I know, but she wanted me to accept the offer as though it was truth. But it's an illusion. Whatever she brought back would be something that could never be my mate, even if he had his physical attributes."

I close my eyes. Lilandra is always there for us. I never thought she could be that lonely in her own life. "You never told me that you miss him that much."

She kisses my cheek. "It's my burden to bear... since it's partly my fault that he was killed. If he hadn't followed me that day, if I hadn't gotten overconfident, maybe I could have been more careful about my mission and taken it seriously." She takes my hand. "You need to understand, we have a lesson to learn, and if we don't do it now, we will have to face it after our death."

I know. I'm in the best position to know. I help so many ghosts into the next life.

"Sorry to interrupt the little chit-chat, but we've got enemies getting closer," Drake says.

"Why me?" I ask. Why did she pick me?

Lilandra smiles at me. "I will tell you when we get back. Stay focused – you know what it's at stake." She squeezes my hand and then releases it.

I unsheathe my katana, already wrapping it in a battle-worthy magic spell.

"I hope that both of you are ready to do this." Drake's sounds excited, and he has a grin in his voice.

I shake my head. Lilandra is right. We will have plenty of time after we make it back to the coven. With my other hand, I draw my gun from its holster.

"What's coming?" I ask.

Drake winks at me. "The way I see it, I will have another demon to kill. There's certainly another werewolf, maybe a couple of witches. At least six enemies, maybe more, and they didn't lose much time catching up to us. Lucky that the other demon is gone."

I gape at him, speechless. How on earth did he manage to kill a demon? "And Marie?" I ask.

Both of them look around.

Lilandra steps forward. "I think her agenda was different from ours. We'll figure it out later. Our priority is the stones. Remember the first law." Lilandra nods at me.

"Right!" I say.

She's right. I know she is, but, at the same time, too many things are happening at once. I have too many questions. There are too many unknowns.

Drake. I can't explain his strength and power, and it's bothering me.

Marie. Why and where did she disappear?

It's too much to ignore, but now is not the time. The time passed differently here. I can feel it in my magic, and Halloween is so close. There's more going on in this cave than I could have ever guessed.

Drake's yellow eyes glow in the shadows. It's dim, but not dark enough to blind us.

The battle is coming.

THE LADY

"Any news, Selena?" My patience grows thin. I'm seated in my chair behind my big desk. The room is dark, but I can see all of Montreal from my place.

She turned toward me. "The second team entered the cave, but the magic surrounding the location blocked our ability to watch inside. We can only wait."

I close my eyes. I'm impatient right now. I want – no, *need* – results and quickly. The plan is coming to a breaking point. All of us need to be prepared. Well, I must be ready. Then we will see who will survive and which of those will pledge themselves to my rule.

"We took a great risk in retrieving that stone. We sent so many inside," I murmur. When I glance at her, she doesn't meet my gaze. I know that my appearance is grotesque, and it will never heal. I live in the shadows. Most of my kind believes I am dead, and I intend to leave it that way.

I'm lucky. Selena is only human, but she is wholly devoted to me. She doesn't understand the whole plan, has no inkling of what is about to happen, which suits me well.

She curtsies. "I know, my Lady, but it's the only way to enter that cave, without having a Witch Warrior in our ranks."

"You're right. I know who to blame. That bitch Lilandra should have accepted my gift, instead of casting it aside for Juniper. Those Witch Warriors are more numerous than anyone knows. Juniper will be trouble, and we will need to eliminate her."

Selena studies her tablet.

"What's happening?"

"Why do you think something is wrong?" she asks me.

"Your expression. I've known you for years now, Selena. You don't need to hide anything from me." She is starting to resist me a little, and my influence is fading. I must be more convincing now.

"I'm not hiding, my Lady. You know I owe you my life. Yet I'm trying to understand the whole plan, so I can serve you best, but some pieces are missing." She gestures to the tablet. "You received another message. It's encrypted."

"Send it to me." I grab my laptop and wait for the message to pop up on my screen. "You can leave me, Selena. Keep me informed when they are out of the cave."

She nods and then leaves my office.

When I open the message, the words I've been waiting for appear.

I'm ready. What do you need?

I smirk. The other phase of my plan is beginning. I type in an encrypted response and send the reply.

It will be spectacular.

No one will suspect a thing, not even my supposed ally, as the scheme of my revenge unfolds.

DONOVAN

I trail Jeremy deeper toward the magical cave.

"We need to get the stone back before they leave," he says.

"They will not make it out of here. We won't let them. The Lady sent reinforcements for us. Our prey will be stuck in the middle of the tunnel," I answer him and then break into a run.

"We lost the demon," Sophia says beside me. Her face puckers with worry.

"I know, love. But, with the help of our reinforcements, we'll hit them hard enough to win."

Sophia continues to run with her spell. Lucas and his mate also follow us as we enter the corridor.

"They are right in front of us. They've stopped in their tracks. Oh, I see," Jeremy says, surprised.

I chuckle – he finally noticed the help that we've received.

The fight started without us.

"I knew you would be back, all of you, well, minus that demon," Lilandra yells.

"Lilandra, why don't you worry about helping your mentee instead? Isn't she supposed to be the daughter you never had," I answer. Sophia may not have wanted to take that route with her former best friend, but I'm fed up with all of this. Lilandra needs to stop threatening my mate, and join her mate in the afterlife.

"It's my job to fight all of you. Though, she could do it by herself. I'm not worried. I taught her well. You may witness a few tricks she has up her sleeve. Tonight is Halloween, after all." Lilandra sounds pleased.

Nearby, Juniper fights several demons. She hits a few of them, but they are beating her back. The male fights another demon.

"Well, I hope you're ready to see that child dead in front of your eyes. I want both stones, and I'll kill all of you to get them," I roar. "We will have our rebellion, and we will win it. Freedom for everyone!"

Lilandra starts to cast more guns around her. I can feel the fire burning inside my mate, demanding to get out. She may have been her best friend, but now she's become her worst enemy.

"Freedom, you say. Killing others will never bring freedom, only anarchy and chaos into the world. You will all lose in the end. You will see, maybe too late, that your methods are foolish."

When Lilandra starts to shoot at us, she uses her magic bullets. I spring into battle, and Lucas follows me. Jeremy runs after us.

They will never be able to catch all of us. My priority is the stones, but not at the price of my mate. The rest of our losses will be collateral damage, a price worth the ultimate reward – freedom for all.

The ground cracks around Lilandra.

Lucas's mate controls the earth element which gives my mate plenty of fire and lava to play with.

Sophia smirks at Lilandra. "You should have taken the offer, my old friend."

"You mean your new enemy. Now no more games. No, you will all die, and we will emerge victorious. You're all wrong. All of you," she shrieks. "Your way will never bring freedom. Never!"

I shift into my wolf, giving my beast full control over myself. Together, Lucas and I try to distract Lilandra in order to make her lose concentration and use too much of her magic energy.

"Don't forget you will have a lot on your conscience, Lilandra. You chose *her* over your mate. You chose *her* over everything. I thought you understood, but I was wrong. No more chances. Now you will die," I bellow.

Behind me, my mate conjures one her biggest spells, utilizing the lava under the ground, and my wolf hair rises along my back. A blazing fire forms between the two sides.

Lilandra starts to cast bazooka and heavy machine guns, clearly deciding to match my mate's firepower. Lucas's mate starts to cast her earth element, drawing chunks of dirt out of the ground to knock Lilandra off her feet. Rocks pelt her, and Sophia sends waves of lava after them.

Lilandra casts something to protect herself, and her bazooka launches into the roof of the cave, causing the whole tunnel to shake. More rocks fall from the ceiling. From my vantage point, I can tell everything will collapse.

I trigger my change back into a man. "Sophia, get back," I yell from my human form. "She's going to make everything fall on us. She's going to kill us!" I run toward my mate as bigger pieces crumble from the ceiling, but she stops them. The fire blazes stronger.

"Lilandra!" I hear Juniper screaming in pain. I look around, but all I can see is Lilandra on the ground, with half of her body stuck, crushed beneath a giant rock.

I can smell it.

She's dying. Lilandra is dying, and I want to laugh.

Again, Juniper screams.

Everything starts to flash.

She glares at Lucas's mate as though she thinks she's the one responsible. Lucas launches himself at Juniper, but her katana is too fast. By the looks of it, she's injured but she's pissed as hell.

"No, Lucas." I close my eyes to block out what's about to happen to Lucas.

He will die, and I can't help him or his mate.

"We need to go, Donovan. We'll escape through the other entrance." Jeremy pushes us to move back where we came from.

I look back in time to see Juniper charge toward Lucas's mate. Lucas's lifeless body lies on the ground beside her.

With her katana, Juniper pierces the witch's belly, then sneers and twists her weapon, creating a fatal wound. The witch will never heal from those – and it's for the best, since Lucas is dead.

We run back to our hiding place through a flurry of spells and chants. The sound fills the cave, but we don't look.

I hope the other team succeeds in retrieving those stones.

If not, the Lady will have our heads.

CHAPTER SEVENTEEN

LILANDRA

Fuck. THAT HURTS.

A gigantic stone crushes my ribcage. Juniper screams my name, but my vision starts to blur. My magic shield nullifies some of the weight of the boulder, but it's not enough. I'm wedged under it, clasped so tight it makes it hard to breathe. There's no getting out of this.

I know what will happen; all those years that I continued to live as though he was with me... In a way, Sophia was right. I miss him. Yet I know that if Lady could bring him back, it would have only been a pale copy. Without a body, it's difficult to bring someone back, and the magical cost is very high. It's closer to black magic, which is banned in the witching community.

"Lilandra!" Juniper screams. She's in pain.

I turn my head toward her voice. My mate and I could never conceive a child. It was something I should have expected. Our union was doomed from the beginning. He was my fated mate, true, but I started doubting destiny when a baby didn't come.

It's why I love Juniper so much. She was the light that helped me make it through all these years without him. I had other mentees before, but over the last three years especially, Juniper became the daughter I never had to me.

I've never told her that. Same as I never said anything about my mate or about Sophia.

I want to leave it all behind, to start anew. I study Juniper.

She tries to push the big rock off me, but I know removing it will kill me instantly. I'm too injured to be made well. "Stop, Juniper. It's over."

Juniper shakes her head. "No, no, it's not true. We will bring you back to the coven. The healer will fix you." She starts to push against the rock magically but I use all my lingering magic energy to try to keep it in place.

"Juniper, listen to me," I whisper. I want her to look at me. Directly in my eyes. I know she's avoiding it.

The demon's scream echoes in the tunnel. Drake must have taken care of him. I suspect the mysterious man is her fated mate, but she doesn't know it yet.

"No, Lilandra. You know I'm right."

DRAKE STEPS BESIDE HER, and he considers me. We share a long look, and I whisper, "It's finished for me."

Juniper gazes straight at me, her eyes filling with tears. I smile. I really love that girl. I raise my hand, and I brush her long blond hair out of her face. All the days out in the field make her hair rebel.

"Listen to me, Juniper. Listen carefully," I rasp.

Tears fall down her cheeks.

"You need to bring this to the coven." I remove the ring that's embedded in my skin.

She shakes her head. "No, you bring it to them. You have to be the one."

"Juniper, I love you. You're the daughter I never had. I know that you have questions. When you're back at the coven, in my apartment, you will find a box with all the information you will need."

"Lilandra, you are my only parent. I always wished you were my mother. You can't die here. You need a healer."

"It's finished. You need to protect the ring, and you need to bring it back to the coven. It's the first law of Witch Warriors. Protect the magical object, at all costs. Hold on to what I taught you. Remember everything and find the box. I cast a spell on it to appear for you."

She wipes the moisture from her cheeks, but she gives me a small nod.

My breathing turns difficult. The rattle in my chest tells the truth that Juniper doesn't want to believe. It's finished. I have to suck at the air, drawing it in. It gets harder with each breath that I take.

The noise of combat rages inside the cave. I know that I need to help Drake, give him more time to bring her back safe to the coven. She won't go without a fight. I peer at Drake. "Take care of her. I know now what you are."

Drake sets his jaw. He takes a breath and then begins dragging Juniper away for me. She claws at his hands, kicking and cursing.

I close my eyes, and I conjure my self-destruction spell.

This is my gift to her.

Drake pulls her along the tunnel, and she shrieks my name over and over.

I give her one last long look. I have loved her more than anything. "I love you, Juniper," I whisper.

I place my hand on my shoulder and start my countdown.

I smile, knowing that Juniper will be in good hands. I couldn't have asked for a better mate for her. Not only can I count on Drake, but Celestia will be there, too.

Juniper will mourn my passing, but she will be safe.

The edge of death begins to take me, and darkness clouds my vision. The afterlife is closer than it's ever been.

I turn to the side, and I see him. "My love."

He seems so alive, as he looked when we conquered the world together. My heart flutters.

"It's time, my love," he says. "I was waiting for you to come back to me. I'm so proud of you. You did good to refuse the Lady, and you did even better with Juniper. You will be able to protect her in another way."

My tears fall on my cheek. "I love you so much!"

He kisses my forehead. "Do it. It's time."

He has given me the last bit of energy that I need. I will do what I have to do to protect those that I love and make sure that their mission succeeds.

Juniper screams, and I'm at peace. It blankets me.

I gaze into the eyes of my mate and finish my casting.

I'm free, free to be with him forever.

JUNIPER

I'm beside Lilandra. She smiles, and I gasp. I know what she's about to do.

She cannot. She must not.

"Lilandra," I scream.

My vision blurs, and I can't see her clearly, but I sense Drake behind me. Lilandra tells him something I can't understand.

Drake takes hold of me and starts to pull me from her. I punch him, scratching and clawing at his hands.

"Let me go. Let me go, you asshole," I yell.

But he doesn't look at me. He stares at Lilandra. She's still saying something to him. My brain doesn't register any of it. I can feel the veil of death drawing close to her, and I want to fight it back. Halloween eve is nearly here, so the veil between the living world and the dead beyond is thin. The two are even closer than usually possible.

Drake holds me tight, still drawing me away from my mentor.

Lilandra begins casting and by the way she puts her hand on her shoulder, I know what she's doing. It terrifies me. My heart pounds in my ears.

She turns and speaks to someone else.

I squint, and I see him. It's a man close to her, talking to her, kissing her. Could he be her dead mate? *No!* He can't have her, not yet.

I need Lilandra, I haven't finished my mentorship. She thinks that I'm ready, but I can't be.

I glance around. Enemies bear down on us, but we're closing in on our exit. I take the ring and embed it in my skin. I'm bound to that ring the same way that I'm bound to the stone. I need to bring them both back to the coven, but I want to take Lilandra with us.

I struggle against Drake. I'm sure that the healer can save her.

"Stop fighting, Juniper. She's beyond our help," Drake growls.

I stare at him. Tears roll down my cheeks, and I don't care. I'm furious. How could life be so unfair? I know people die every day, but not like this, not without a proper burial.

I punch him again. Yet his skin is hard. He isn't human.

"Leave me alone. I need to bring her back. We need to save her," I wail. I turn to look at her. *No, no, no...* Not the self-destruction spell. "No! Lilandra, don't do it!"

Drake must have sensed the danger. We are in a cavernous tunnel way underground. Casting self-destruction will bring chaos.

"We need to get out of here," he says as he pushes me toward the other path out of the tunnel.

More enemies are coming, and my anger grows. This is all their fault.

They need to hurt. They need to die. I need to make them suffer for Lilandra, for all those that have lost someone because of them.

"You need to be safe, so we have to get out of here. It's what Lilandra wants," Drake says.

A big explosion shakes the foundations of the earth around us. The whole cave rumbles and rocks crumble to the ground.

"Let's get out of here!" Drake yells at me.

I know in my heart that Lilandra is gone. It makes a void in my heart. I fall on the ground. I don't want to continue. My second mother just destroyed herself for me.

I'm lost again. Only to live my life with dead people, only seeing ghosts.

"No, Juniper. We need to continue, everything will collapse soon. The cave is still standing, but I'm guessing whoever created that place left some kind of safety net that we must use to get out." Drake tries to help me to my feet.

A noise echoes behind us. I look around, and see there are fewer of our enemies now. Lilandra was able to buy us some time, but we have to get out ASAP.

My body aches. I want to scream. I want to hurt someone.

I draw my katana and my guns, but I know what I need to do.

I study Drake as he seems to be weighing our options. The cave still shakes after Lilandra self-destruction spell. He must be right about the safety spell.

I graze the ground and I feel it: the invisible veil, the wall between worlds. My mother had told me that combining my father's Witch Warrior side with her ability to interact with the spirit world would bring me a unique magic, some kind of power that only I would have.

A lot of people died here, Lilandra included. Now I know what has to be done.

I place my hand on the ground and start to cast my spirit spell. I never called for a spirit to come to me or to fight for me, but now it's different. Now I need them. This is my wild card. I need to put all the enemies down and flee from the cavern. I must make it back to the coven, so Lilandra will not have died in vain.

I look at Drake and smile at him. The spell could take all my magic energy, and I don't know how that will affect my body, but now is not the time to overthink.

"I'm calling all the good spirits of this land. All of you, I summon you to join me. To help me. I'm calling for help. I'm calling on you all, to help me protect these magical artifacts."

I continue my casting. I need an army, and it comes: through the veil, like a curtain ready to be thrown back, I feel the spirits as if they are right beside me, some of them hovering on the other side of the divide.

They are real for me. They are part of me. I'm the conduit who needs them, but they also need me, need to be useful.

On the ground beside me, my hand starts to glow as the magic circle forms in front of me. An element rises. It gusts like the wind. It's strong, so strong. I never felt something like this before, never had that kind of power. I begin to understand what my mother was teaching me before both of my parents disappeared and left me alone in the world.

My magic energy is boosted on this day. It's the only day of the year that both worlds could coexist for the night only.

DRAKE

We are surrounded. I need to take my mate to safety. More enemies are coming, and I don't know what Lilandra did, but I know she is dead. I feel my mate's sorrow and despair. She lost someone important today.

I glance at my mate. "Come, Juniper, we need to..."

Before I can finish, she places her hand on the ground, and she's casting.

I frown. But what on earth is she casting?

Goosebumps rise on my skin. This is not good. A circle starts to form, and my mate is surrounded by her light. The wind whirls in a circle around her. Her hair flies from side to side. Her eyes, her gorgeous eyes disappear and are replaced by wholly white orbs.

The ground cracks, and I can see them, spirits, so many ghosts surrounding my mate. Her face changes, too.

This is necromancy. It's hard to believe, but that must be what it is.

She's talking to them as if they are alive. Lilandra told me that Juniper was special. I suspect she's more than a Witch Warrior.

This is not magic. This is so much more.

My life energy that her magic is amplified but also depleting quickly. That spell is getting all of her magical resources, which means that she could die or lose conscious-ness at any moment. The first option is not a possibility. I won't let it happen. I must make her safe. My beast had his fun, but now it's serious. He wants to come out to protect her, but the confines are too close for that.

"We need those magic items," one of the enemies calls, gesturing to the others. "All of you, go get it!"

One of them yells, and leads them all into a charge toward us.

I need to think... and fast. Juniper's arms start shaking. The casting seems to have drained a lot of her magic energy, which means I only have one choice: I must bring her back to the coven.

But how? She won't be able to teleport us.

The enemies don't seem to see all the ghosts, but I do, which confirms the fact that Juniper is my mate.

Her spirit army engages the enemy, and soon enough, the werewolf's cry pierces the cacophony of battle – clearly, the spirits can hurt them even if they are invisible.

I run toward my mate. My options are limited, but I have to do something.

"Drake." *That* voice.

I look aside and see Lilandra. She smiles at me. "Take her. I know what you are and you don't have to hide anymore. We need you. She needs you. She may not know it right now, but, since you are her mate, she will always need you. Free yourself and be yourself."

I take my mate in my arms, and I unleash my beast. I know how strong we are, which will give the spirits more time to do what needs to be done. The cave starts to crumble beneath the weight of my beast as I scoop Juniper into my arms. I release my head and start to spit fire around my me, to help free myself from this place and dig a hole through which we could escape.

My dragon starts to do the work.

"What's that?" one of the enemies asks.

I don't have time for them; I push and smash against the roof of the cave until it gives. As I set us free from the ground, I unfurl my wings and take off into the sky. I will return Juniper to the coven so she can heal, and finish that mission for her.

CHAPTER EIGHTEEN

DONOVAN

WE DART INTO ANOTHER BRANCH OF THE CAVE AS THE ground shakes. Jeremy chases after us, dodging falling rocks and stones.

"Impossible!" Sophia says, stopping short.

I raise my eyebrow. "What is it, love?"

She closes her eyes and a single tear rolls down her cheek. I take her face in my hands, studying her. What could be wrong?

When she opens her eyes again, moisture fills her eyes, and she blinks. She's trying so hard to be strong. She doesn't want to cry.

"She's dead," she whispers.

"Well, love. We saw it. It was easy to see her time was up."

She frowns at me. "You don't understand. One thing Witch Warriors are taught to use is a self-destruct spell. It makes them different than most other magic users. That's why the cavern is falling down on our heads. I don't think the rest of the team made it."

I look back the way we came. Our surroundings are still rumbling from that implosion. "Lilandra did that?"

She nods. "We need to leave fast. This place is going to collapse as soon as the magic protecting it fails, and I don't know how long that will take."

I pull her close, and we rush toward the end of the tunnel and the light, but Jeremy can't go out into the real sunlight. He needs to stay inside and dig a hole, and we will have to wait until night time so we can leave.

Jeremy busies himself, digging a spot to hide.

Sophia casts a shield spell. "It's just something to protect him from rocks and debris."

We both stare at the blue sky. It's been so many days since we've seen the real one.

"Blessed be, my friend. I know we weren't on the same side, but I will always have you in my heart." Sophia says out loud. It's a side of the witches that I don't understand. They might be enemies, but they still respect one another.

I point to a shadowy shape in the sky. "Look at that."

"Is that a dragon?" Sophia asks.

I finally understand. "Yes, he is — the only one who could defeat a demon."

She turns toward me. "You mean that man that follows Juniper and protects her?"

I nod. "He is a shifter, which only means that Juniper is his mate. That's why he defeated a demon — dragons are the strongest shifters on this planet. If my assumption is right, he's probably very old, which gives him even more strength."

They left Lilandra behind, and Juniper's mission could be the only reason for that. That probably meant we failed, and that both artifacts will soon be in the hands of the coven.

The Lady will not be happy, but how could we have known that a dragon shifter would get involved? I would never have guessed it. We need to get back when night falls and Jeremy can travel. We need to regroup. I'm pretty sure the Lady will not stop until she gets the objects... which also means she will have another mission for us.

"It's not finished," Sophia sighs.

"I know, love." I hug her. I need to rest. She does, too. "We will make camp here," I say. "It's not the hotel, but we all need our rest."

She nods, and we get to work.

We are fighting for the right side. We will succeed in our rebellion. All factions will collapse and only the unification of all races will prevail. It must be so. At all costs.

She put her arms around me, and we decide to sleep.

MARIE

Ah, there it is.

I close my mind. Certainly, I have my own agenda. But I'm not the enemy, so why does my heart feel as though I am betraying them? My mission is clear. I need to bring back that box that was stolen from us by the witches centuries ago.

I need to bring it back to my Queen. I have information she needs to know too. I have a feeling that something is going on, something way much bigger than us.

The ground starts to shake so much that I almost lose my footing. I grab the box as my instincts scream at me to leave, to flee. I hope that my friends are safe. Maybe I will be able to see them again. I pray that they will forgive me for leaving them.

I form my portal to report back.

"Do you have news?" One of the Queen's advisors asks me.

"I have the object, and I'm heading back to the manor."

The advisor's eyes widen slightly. "I will tell her."

I close the portal. I hope that my weird feeling is wrong, but I felt that something big just happened with that earthquake. My mission is done. Now I need to head back and take one of the other tunnels which I noticed were clear and close by.

The roof of the cave that replaced the sky for so long is starting to crack. That cannot be good.

I start to run and don't look back. I have to make the plane back to Montreal. The faster I can, the better. I know that my Queen already has plans for me, and I'll have to head back to the airport.

"See you, my friends." I say out loud. "Maybe we are destined to see each other sooner rather than later."

I leave the island and climb into the nearest taxi as soon as I'm able. What is going on? What is all this? I believe that it's way bigger than any of us, and we will have to get involved at some point. Once I'm on the plane, I start to relax in the private jet that my Queen requested for me.

I'm safe. Faeries own the plane, and I'm safe. I drift to sleep, determined to find out if they are all alive.

THE LADY

We just received the report.

I close my eyes. Those fucking Witch Warriors are in my way all the time. No, it's not them — it's the Supernatural Intelligence Agency.

I kick Selena out of my office. I don't want to see anyone. Least of all her.

Minutes later, my private phone beeps, and I take the call, placing the phone to my ear.

"So, did you succeed?" she asks.

I don't answer. I really want to smash something right now.

"Twin, silence is so unlike you when things are going well," the voice on the other end of the line says.

"I'm not in the mood right now. We lost two artifacts to those witches. I need more. I need more power."

My sister sighs on the phone. "I know. But let's face it, we need to divide their forces. If they have to look for different objects, they will not be able to work together."

I take a seat at the window and stare at the city beyond. "What did you have in mind?"

"I think you need me on your team right now," she says. "I could manage the faeries' faction. There are plenty of things I could do without being noticed. After all, I'm part of the Queen's court."

I remain silent, but my brain goes into overdrive. "You would do that for me? I thought being a part of the Faerie's court was important to you."

"Sis, you're my priority. What they did to you, they also did to me. Faerie twins are special, you know that. I could feel what they did to you. I may not have those scars, but that doesn't mean that I couldn't feel them on my skin."

I jump to my feet and begin pacing. "What did you say?"

"I know that you are trying to make the SIA: Special Operations Team work on Gorad the Black case right now. They don't know you're attempting to distract them. You're working your ass off for the rest of the factions, but I know you haven't touched the faeries' faction yet. You are using your team to enact your revenge. Let me take care of the faeries' faction. This will draw the SIA: Investigation Team, too. I want them to suffer like you did. I stay here, but the way that I see it, they are beginning to notice something is wrong. They sent someone with the Witch Warriors on a retrieval mission." My sister pauses. When she speaks again, her voice is excited. "It's the box."

"What? Are you telling me the box was there?"

"THE WAY I UNDERSTAND IT, YES," she replies.

" I knew that box was stolen, but I never thought it was the witches that did it. Damn. I need it."

"Yes, I suspected you would want it. Let me work on that, and I will report back to you. I got myself a good team here. They're against the Queen. This will help us in the end."

"Do it. Stay safe," I tell my sister. Then I hang up.

That box is the origin of the faeries' magic. There's nothing better for my revenge on the faeries. Suddenly, I'm in the best mood I've been in for days.

My revenge is shaping up nicely.

~

DRAKE

I'm waiting for my mate to wake up.

The healers are still helping her. I brought her back with no time to spare.

"Thank you for bringing her back."

I jump at the voice of a young lady ghost who stands right in front of me. "Hmmm. You're a spirit."

She laughs. "My name is Celestia. I'm a close friend of Juniper. I help her with her other side and sometimes I'm able to find the information she needs. The medium side of her is strong today, and the veil between is very thin, but at midnight, that will stop. You're able to see me because of this, but also because she cast a big spell."

I nod. I've never conversed with a ghost before. I'm

centuries old, and I have had more surprises than since my mate entered my life.

Celestia peers at me. She seems to be from another time, not like the teenagers of these days. "You're special, too."

"What is your story?" I ask her.

"What do you mean?"

"Well, by the way you dress, I can tell that you are not from this time. You're young enough that you are not married. At the same time, you seem old."

She smiles at me, but she doesn't answer. The door to the healers' triage room opens, and one old man walks out toward me.

"How is she?" I ask.

"She's fine right now. It took four healers to help me. I don't know what kind of spell she did, but it almost drained all of her Witch Warrior magic. In her case, it is very strong. We have someone in there to help her recovery, and we've called the Librarian to take the magical objects back to her vault."

"Can I see her?" I ask.

The old healer shuffles uncomfortably, as if wondering how he's going to prevent me from entering anyway. "Usually, only close family and mentor are allowed inside."

"That's fine, Ginger. He is her mate. I thought the dragon shifters disappeared centuries ago."

I know that I'm older than him, but physically I'm close to thirty. "I slept for centuries, but I woke up a decade ago, for a reason I didn't understand. I assure you, I'm not the only one that remains, but some forgot to wake up, or are taking their time to do it."

"Elder, what is he?" Ginger was her name as him.

"Well, you didn't see him landing with Juniper. He is a shifter dragon, a very old one, older than me if I could guess."

Ginger seems shocked. "They were extinct."

"Well, I can tell you that I'm alive and well. Also, I'm not the only one."

"You were with Juniper?"

I nod. "Yes, if you're asking about the cave inside of that island that seems full of magic at some point, yes."

The Elder came close to me. "For sure, we will need to debrief Juniper, but it will be useful to hear your account. Could you describe your experience with everything that has happened since you started following Juniper?" The Elder asks, then he starts to walk, inviting me to join him.

I glance at the door where Juniper is under healer care, but he calms me down. "She will be there when we are back. Don't worry."

I can smell that she's out of danger. "Fine, let's go for a walk." Others join us as we go.

I start to explain how I discovered Juniper entering the cave. How I knew she was my mate, and all the traps, and how Lilandra came to join us with Marie.

"Wait, you're telling me a faerie was with her?"

"Yes, she wasn't with us to begin with. Lilandra told us that everything was fine, and that we should let it go. We went through a few fights together, and then we found where the stone was hidden, inside another cave. Then Marie the faerie disappeared without telling us anything."

The Elder thinks a moment. "Not good."

I stop walking. "Okay, tell me why, old man."

"Please, sir, have a little bit of respect," one of the witches with him lectures me.

"That's fine," the man says. "I suppose he is older than me. How many?"

I smirk. "How many what?"

He starts to laugh. "Years you've lived, if not centuries."

I snort and scrutinize him. "I stopped counting two centuries ago."

"That's what I thought," he says, "older than me, but you still look like you're in your thirties."

"Well, once I find my mate, I'll stay like this, that way I can grow older with her. Now why is it bad that the faerie left us?" I ask the Elder.

"Well, from what I know, many centuries ago, a group of witches stole the faeries' box which contains the lost story of their magic."

"Sorry. Did you say they lost their magic? The last time I checked, they still had it." The story doesn't make any sense.

"They do, but the box contains a higher level of magic that was lost centuries ago. We kept it because the faeries' magic was becoming too strong. They were starting to think they were the boss of all of us."

I begin to understand — in order to protect everything, they started a war with them. "I guess that not a lot of people know that."

"True, but I think that will have to change. If what I suspect is true, and the intel I've started receiving from inside the cave is correct... The box is gone. With Marie being gone, I can only assume her mission was to retrieve it and use all of you in the process."

I look at him. "Well, that will not change the fact that the enemy is striking against all factions, which includes faeries."

"I agree." The Elder stops talking and peers back from where we came through narrowed eyes. "Ah, I suspect that Juniper is waking up now. Good luck."

I look back as well. One of the healers coming toward us. Now I need to make Juniper understand that she's my mate. My beast and I suspect this will be the most difficult part of all.

CHAPTER NINETEEN

JUNIPER

Slowly, I return from the darkness.

I know my spell worked. I saw her one last time, but not for long, just a flash. She spoke to Drake, and I couldn't make any sense of what she said. I shudder as anguish rushes through me.

My mentor, my second mother is gone. No body to be buried. Nothing. Only my memories and all the things she taught me for almost a decade now.

I don't move. Not yet. I try to make my brain work. I feel my magic flowing again. The spell almost drained me. My real mother had been concerned about the mix that I had in me. She was right. It could consume me completely.

"Well, I will say she's lucky: not only is he handsome, but he is also a dragon shifter. He seems so powerful," someone in the room says, a woman talking to someone else, I think.

"He is her mate," the other one answers. "It's so romantic to fly your mate back home in your dragon form."

What? What are they saying?

I try to remember what Lilandra said to him to help us escape, but I only remember being protected by him. Though, in hindsight, he was big. My memory is not fully back yet, and I need to recuperate. The only thing that I am able to understand is that Lilandra is gone forever.

"Oh, I see that you're awake," says the red-haired healer.

I smile at her as she comes into my room. The other two scurry out without another word.

"Yes, I am." I move to sit up on my bed.

"Be careful," she says. "We almost lost you. I don't know what kind of spell you did, but that's a freakishly strong one."

I grin. Though, I don't want to talk about this. The only person that I could talk to isn't there anymore. "I know. I can feel it in my body. I'm drained, almost. Can I go home?"

"No, the Elder will arrive soon with Drake."

I glare at her. "I don't want to see him."

"You have no choice. The Elder needs to hear both your stories."

True, there's always a debriefing after a mission. Since I'm stuck at the hospital, I guess that will be done here. But I don't have time to ask any more questions as both the healer and Drake enter the room.

Drake's eyes are on me, for a reason I don't understand. I begin to feel small and vulnerable at one point.

A lot of people think the Elders are just weird witches or wizards, but they all mean well and take care of all the magic users that are part of the witch faction.

"Ah, my child, I'm so happy that you are back with us," the Elder says.

"They said that I can't go to my room yet. That you need to talk to me," I answer.

He smiles. "You're straight to the point, my child. True, you know that debriefing should have happened already, but

Drake told us the whole story since he was with you most of the mission."

I look toward Drake. He's standing at the foot of my bed, and the Elder takes the chair to sit beside me.

"Yes, we were together along with Lilandra and Marie. Now Lilandra is dead, and Marie is missing. I got the two magic objects, though. Where are they?"

The Elder takes my hand. "Don't worry, the Librarian came and picked them up. She knows about Lilandra. They knew each other well. It seems that Lilandra helped his cousin get a spot at the Paranormal University."

It makes me happy to hear it. Though, it makes me miss her more. Lilandra was always helping people: that made her who she was.

I nod. I don't want to talk much about this. I don't know if my emotions can handle it.

"Now I know what you are," the Elder says. "The spell that you cast was not a true Witch Warrior spell. I did some digging on your mother's side. All of them, mostly the female side of the family, had the ability to see ghosts and interact with them. Combine that gift with the potent magic power of your father, and it could be a great asset for you."

I stop breathing a second. I always thought that power was wrong to begin with.

"You seem surprised, my child."

I study them both: even Drake seems fine with this. My voice shakes when I speak. "Well, during the time that I had with my mother, she always told me to be careful with my gift. Not everyone would understand. Some people want it and that could have made me a target for evil people when I was young."

The Elder pats my hand. "That's fine. With everything that's coming, you will have to start to work with those powers. They will be very useful."

Drake clears his throat. "Don't worry. I'll make sure she never empties her magic."

I almost forgot about Drake, almost.

I glare at him. "Why do you think there will be a next time? You're not part of our coven. You're a shifter that people won't shut up about. An attractive dragon shifter."

The Elder coughs at my words. "I'm too old for this. Denying yourself the gift of mating is wrong, and you know that, child." He begins to lecture me.

I smirk at Drake. "But different factions can't mingle that way. It's against the laws."

"Well, we have started to have discussions on this. At one time, we thought that was our salvation. Now, with all the different kinds of mating bonds that are appearing naturally, we think that belief might be incorrect. I can't stop him from following you, Juniper, and even if I tried to prevent him, he probably could kill all of us."

I frown at him. The Elders are the oldest beings inside the faction. They are older than some vampires.

"Sorry, I mean no disrespect, but you're older than him, aren't you?" I ask.

He rises from his chair. "Well, Juniper, I can tell that he is older than me."

At that, he leaves my room. Drake stays behind, watching me like a hawk.

Older than an Elder? That's impossible. Drake looks thirty.

~

DRAKE

She doesn't want to look at me.

"You can leave, you know. I'm fine now," she says.

I snort. "Well, what can I say? You're stuck with me." I take the Elder's place in the seat. I study her. Her long blond hair is a mess, but I stare into her big blue eyes. "Why do you think I followed you back from your mission?" I didn't want to sound like a lecture, but I couldn't do otherwise.

If her eyes were surprised before, now anger flashes in them. "You're a pain in my ass right now. I don't know what Lilandra told you, but I'm relieving you of whatever it was that you promised her."

I smile at her, loving the fact that she doesn't know how to deal with me. That's good. I want her on edge, these missions of hers are not the best or easiest for me at my age. Though, the way I see it, I have no choice in the matter.

"I didn't promise anything to her. I do what needs to be done."

Her brows draw together.

Good. She doesn't understand yet.

"Why are you here and why do you seem to want to follow me everywhere?"

I notice the ring on her wedding finger. I touch it. I can feel it. Only my mate could wear that ring, but I don't know how it's come to be in her possession.

"The ring is yours?" I ask.

She looks at her finger, tracing the dragon on the ring. "Yes, it belongs to me."

"Only my mate could wear it or find it."

She blinks twice in surprise. "What?"

"You heard me. Why do you think I kissed you? That starts the bonding for us shifters. But you know your research. You know about all this."

She flushes at my statement. "If you think you can come here, act like a caveman and claim me, you've got the wrong girl."

Much better. I like her like this. I love her spirit. She

never gives up. "I didn't say anything like that, but if you want me to, I can." I wiggle my eyebrows at her.

She throws a punch at me, but misses.

I laugh with satisfaction. "You better not be after me. We're not bonded yet. I haven't had any wet dreams, and believe me, mating dreams can be quite... incredible."

Her eyes bulge. "Maybe, but that doesn't change the fact. Don't forget that the last time we slept, it was under Lilandra's spell."

When I say that name, Juniper's face changes. She's been surprised and mad, but now she's sad. Her eyes start to water, and she hides her gaze from me. I stay silent. She's not ready yet.

"Can you leave me alone now?" she asks. I'm going back to my apartment for a while."

I can't force our bonding on her, but nature will take its course as it should.

I nod. "I will let you be, but if you leave, I will hunt you down. In a way, I hope you do, because my dragon loves to hunt."

Her eyes widen, but I can't tell if it's surprise, shock, or fury.

I decide to leave her. She needs time for herself. I want to comfort her, but I can't force that on her either.

"She will be difficult, but she will understand one day. Need a place to stay?" the Elder asks. He's waiting for me outside the room to give us privacy.

When I nod to the Elder, he walks me to a small apartment. By the smell, it must be right beside Juniper's.

∾

JUNIPER

A few healers help me back to my apartment, supporting me as I walk. Once inside, they tell me that I should call them back if I need more healing.

But all I want is to be alone. I need to wrap my head around everything that's happened. Not only is Lilandra gone, now that caveman tells me I'm supposed to be his mate.

He is bluffing. Of that, I'm sure.

"You're back!"

I turn to my favorite teenager. "Celestia, it's good to see you. How are things around here?"

Celestia wants to say something, but she seems unsure.

"You can ask me anything," I offer.

She peers at me with her ghostly eyes. "Is it true?"

"About Lilandra?"

She nods.

"Yes, it's true, she's gone. Did you see her?"

"No, but I felt something during that night. You know that the veil was so thin. I could feel that something was wrong, I thought it was you. I'm relieved it wasn't, and but, at the same time, I'm sad."

Suddenly, a big box appears on my kitchen table, surrounded with dark blue magic. I know that magic signature, and all those Celtic and other designs on it. I recall what Lilandra said to me. The box is magically hidden and can only be revealed to me when she dies.

"What's this?" Celestia asks.

"Apparently, it's a box that Lilandra kept for me for after her death." Do I have the energy to go through it? I suspect that if I don't open it, the container will haunt me all night, but I want to be alone when I do. We both stare at it.

"I saw your mate," Celestia says out of the blue.

"What?"

"That dragon shifter."

"How do you know that he is my mate?"

Celestia sighs. "Well, because that ring belongs to him and his energy is starting to intertwine with yours."

I don't want to answer at all. I'm tired, sore, and all I want is to stay under my covers and let all of my pain loose.

"Oh, I can see that you want to be alone," she says.

I give her a weak smile.

She approaches me and kisses my forehead. I sense her energy.

"I will be here if you need me," she says. Then she leaves me the same way she came.

All ghosts decide to appear or not. I'm sure she's close, but doesn't want to bother me.

I approach the box. I don't know how long she prepared for this. I feel the last of her magic energy, swirling in the air around the box. When I reach for it, I realize that I'm trembling.

I shake my head and force myself to open it. At my touch, the lock comes undone. She knew that I would not want to open the box — the fact that the lock unfastened and the lid opened the moment I touched it meant that she knew that I would want put it somewhere else. I swallow hard, my lower lip starting to quiver. Her energy surrounds me, and all I can hear is her voice.

Dear Juniper,

If you receive this box, it's because I'm no longer living. I probably made sure that no one could bring me back. Don't be sad. I will join him again.

A decade has gone since he passed away, a decade of guilt has washed through me. Now I'm at peace. One of the things that helped me get through all those years alone was all my mentees, but since you became a part of my life a couple of years ago, you became the most important.

You will have all that belongs to you. My will is secure in the Librarian's vault. I don't have many belongings — most will disappear except the box — but I do have treasure in the vault with the will. I know that you can be a hothead sometimes, but learn how to control it, Juniper. You're possibly one of the strongest Witch Warriors, and I suspect that you will need that control.

I should have died with him, or sometimes I wonder if I should have accepted Donovan's gift. You have the right to learn about my best friend, Sophia. She is not my enemy. She's a fire witch, a very strong one. I never guessed that her mate was a werewolf. They presented me with an irresistible offer: to give them back the Seal in exchange for my mate's resurrection. I knew that was impossible, but a part of me wants him back so much that it hurts my body and wounds my magic.

I decided to do otherwise. I decided to be there for my mentees, but mostly for you. I never got the chance to have children with him, so I always thought of you as the daughter that I never had and probably never will have. I know you lost your parents very young. You were so in need of love, and your anger got you in trouble more than once.

I know about Drake and what he is.

At least I'm leaving here knowing that Drake will be with you. You will have the chance to be loved for real and not to worry about losing it at the end because life decides to be unfair with you.

My time is up, I don't regret any choices that I have made. The only thing that I regret was losing him. Don't be stubborn, Juniper, as I know you can. Drake is your mate.

Live your life, my special adopted daughter. Be happy and don't let all the anger consume you. You're not a freak. You're special. I love you and will always love you. Let him into your heart, and you will not regret it at all.

I love you. Stay safe, your time is not here yet.

Lilandra Reeves

WITH THAT, the voice fades and all the magic that swirls in my room goes also. I look inside the box, but my vision is blurry with tears. Carefully, I lift the Celtic cross necklace that belonged to her. I always wondered why she didn't wear it anymore. Now I know. I take the necklace and place it around my neck.

I could feel her, her energy, in the necklace, and it crashes through my last defense. I collapse on my bed and let all my tears flow. I let the pain pour from me. My adoptive mother just left me, and I will never be able to put my arms around her again.

CHAPTER TWENTY

DRAKE

MY MIND FILLS WITH JUNIPER... HER HAIR, HER EYES, EVERY part of her. My dragon smacks his lips, and desire overcomes me. I will have her.

I'm stuck on my bed without my mate, but my room fills with the sense of her. The kiss is beginning to bind us together, but she doesn't notice it yet. Through the connection, I can feel her pain. My dragon and I bleed for her. All we want is to be with her, to comfort her. But she will never let us do it.

"I know what you are," a girl whispers behind me.

When I turn around, the little teenager stands there. With the binding underway for Juniper and me, the spell she cast makes me see and feel things I couldn't see before. My dragon sees, too. Somehow, we're viewing the world through Juniper's abilities.

"I see you're still here?" I say, studying the ghostly young lady.

She smiles. "Most of the dead ones are. A lot of people

would forget about us. But those who don't want to cross or are not ready to cross stay behind. Yet we all want to learn, understand, and gain experiences that we missed out on in our life. At least the ones that remain behind."

"Do you have a name?"

"Juniper calls me Celestia... I think it's my name from when I was alive." She seems so young, but her words aren't young at all.

"Do you remember how you died?" I ask.

She shakes her head. "Juniper thinks that means something wasn't solved or finished in my life, so it blocks my path to the afterlife. "

I look at the wall between Juniper and me. My heart aches for her.

"That ring belongs to you?" she asks.

I glance at her. "Yes, it does. I don't know how she got it."

She grins at me. "That's my fault, I suppose. But I knew it belonged to her. Its energy called to her. I gave it to her just before she left for Scotland to answer the call of the Stone of Destiny."

"I thought I lost it centuries ago." I smile. Part of me is happy that Juniper got my ring.

"Odd that you don't ask me how I got the ring."

I chuckle. "No, In my experience, magic energy is strange, and it finds ways to do the impossible." I could ask how Celestia found it, but I like puzzles, and I want to unravel the mystery of Juniper on my own.

"You're right, Drake. I am not going to give you details — only if Juniper asks. I know she's usually curious, but now she needs time for herself."

I sigh at Celestia's statement. "Did you visit her?"

She nods. "She asked me to leave, but she knows we're still around. We're just invisible. All spirits and ghosts decide if they want to be seen. The only exception is when Juniper's power pierces the veil between the spirit and human world, which was thin last night. She has power, but it's one hell of a spike in her magic on that night."

I definitely have questions about her powers and gifts, but, in a way, I want Juniper to share this with me. I want her to trust me with that. I want her to be the one to tell me.

Celestia leans toward me. "She will not surrender to you, you know that."

I laugh. "Yes, I expect as much. She will give me the chase of my life. That's fine. It'll make our union that much sweeter. My beast and I are happy to give chase."

She looks at me or, more like, she looks through me.

"Is something wrong?" I ask, a little nervous about her intensity.

She giggles. "No, but I can tell by your energy or, like some humans call it, your aura, that your bond with her has started forming already. What did you do during the mission?"

"Not much besides keeping her alive all the time. She manages to get herself into a lot of trouble most of the time."

She crosses her arms. "Well, why don't I believe that's all you did?"

"Why don't you believe me? I'm disappointed you think that I would take advantage of her."

She laughs. "I don't really think that. I guess you're very old, to know people and how they behave so well."

"True, but I also slept for centuries before I woke up a couple of years ago. I suspect I woke when she grew old enough to call for her mate."

Celestia puts one finger on her cheek while she thinks. "Maybe. I know that faith brought you awake for her and for you too. You need her, both you and your dragon."

· · ·

I DON'T ANSWER. I don't have to. She's right. One thing I know is that dragon shifters can sleep for decades, even centuries. But when our mate is close to mating age, we wake up. My inner beast craves Juniper in a way a simple man never could.

I lean back and put my hands behind my head. "She can't escape me. That kiss I gave her will bring our magic energies together. Our two parts are already fusing, beginning to turn into one. I will be able to find her anywhere."

She nods at me. "You know she will flee. She'll run as hard and as fast as she can."

I smile. "Well, if she does, I will be right behind her, never very far from her."

"I'm happy she found someone. Even if she doesn't know it yet. It's not good for her to be close to the dead. Since Lilandra is dead, that means Juniper will find her. Juniper needs those in the land of the living, also."

At that, Celestia starts to fade. She's right. It's a big loss for Juniper. Lilandra and Juniper were close. I learned that Juniper's parents died when she was young. Life gave her Lilandra to be the missing parent figure, at a time when they both needed each other. Now Juniper has her coven and her job, but she also has me. I hope that will be enough to keep her tied to the land of the living.

I lie back on the bed and stare at the ceiling. Sleep claims me slowly, but I know that my dragon is there to watch and wake me if need be.

~

JUNIPER

I'm running in the woods. I use a speed spell to run faster, and I laugh as the wind rushes over me. I'm happy and turn to glance over my shoulder. Something is following me.

"If you think you can hide from your mate, you're wrong." The deep, rough voice cuts through the silence around me. I can't see the speaker, but he is in my head.

I look up and I see him. His beast, the dragon, is flying above me.

"I know I can, and I will." I continue to cast my running spell. He descends, coming closer to me. The downdraft from his wings disturbs the air around me. I push my casting further. I won't give into him easily. Heat rolls off him, this beast on top of me. A moment later, his human form lands on me and knocks me to the ground.

I don't cry out. I laugh instead.

"Gotcha!" he yells. I roll over in his arms. He smiles, his face only inches from mine. "You know I love to chase you. You may cast, but we will always be right behind you. We'll find you." He kisses me, hard. His lips sear my own, burning the tender places. He's branding me. He will always be there. I want to lean into him, to draw him into me. But he pulls away.

I wink. "You can't be mad at me for trying."

"Oh, you can try, but be sure I will always find you. Anywhere you run." He kisses me again. He's teasing me, and I like it. I never thought I would have a mate, and now I understand what Lilandra wanted to teach me so many years ago. Thinking of her makes me sad and happy at the same time. I know she's with her mate — that's one of the reasons she never visits me.

Drake peers into my face. "Hey, what are you thinking?" he asks, gently.

I give him a weak smile. "Lilandra."

He strokes my hair. "Are you okay?"

I nod. "It's mostly happy thoughts. Back then, as her student, I never understood the mating thing, even though she tried to explain it to me. But now I know exactly what it feels like."

He gives me a big smile, and his dimples appear. Each time he flashes those at me, I die and go to heaven. Everything I have ever wanted, I see in them.

"I'm happy, my beloved mate," he says. "With all those centuries without one, or a reason to wake and live my life, I know I was waiting for you."

I grab his cheeks and bring his lips against mine. I want all those lost centuries to be out of his life. I want to feel him against me. I move my hips against his. My body starts to shake in a convulsion.

He pulls me closer, his face twisted in worry. "Not again?"

Another one, a big one. He starts to fade, and lightning flashes around me.

Juniper, come to me. Save me. Protect me. They want me. I'm the stone of the god, and I'm not ready to be released yet. I register the surrounding call.

A relic stone calls to me.

"Where are you and what are you?" I ask.

"The lightning will help you in your quest. Only the god of thunder can have me. You must protect me from all others. That creature is not a goddess, even if she believes she is."

The god of lightning, Zeus, is the only one that should wield the stone of thunder, and the stone is calling for my help.

"Where are you?" I ask once more.

"Go. Travel north to my people. Meet with those who worshipped us in the past."

W ITH A JOLT, I wake up in my bed. Yet my body still hums with desire. My breath rages. Another call from another relic. But I just returned. That dream started like a regular one, but at the same time, it asked me to go back on mission. I look at Lilandra's box. I am drained, but the jolt tells me otherwise.

I get up and head to the bathroom. I need to do a little research. The stone wasn't very clear about anything.

"You're up!" her little voice announces.

I jump a little. I look at Celestia's ghostly form. "Yes." My body trembles once more.

"What?" she exclaims. "You've already got another call. You just got back. Can't you take any vacation at all?"

I smile. I needed her sass this morning. All my emotions are all over the place. I need her way of seeing things. "I don't think magical objects know about vacations. Neither do the people always grabbing relics. They should put vacations in their evil contracts somewhere," I tell her.

She laughs. "That's an excellent one. Beside all this with the relic, what are you going to do about him?"

I snarl. "Do I really have to do something about him?"

She rolls her eyes, annoyed. "Well, he is your mate. You can't ignore it."

"I will do my job, and my job only. What would I do with a mate? I'm not a very social person to begin with. I like being alone. Mates tend to mess that up. Do you really see me with a male that will tell me what I can and cannot do?"

She sighs. "You need to grow up. You know that."

I grin. "A teenager told me to grow up. Really?"

She slaps me — well, her hand passes through me, but I know she's frustrated right now. "You're a baby," she says. "I may not have much experience with love and relationships, but I've seen plenty of them. You dream of him, too, his energy surrounded you."

My cheeks burn. "Don't tell me that I have been talking in my sleep again?"

She smiles. "No, but I can tell in the aura and you know it. I guess you can't see your own aura. It tells the truth even when you won't." She pauses. "You like him."

I nod. It's true. I'm not only a Witch Warrior but also a medium, as the human world calls it. It also means that I can read the auras of each person or being I meet. They are all different.

She gestures to my hand. "Still, you are not able to remove the ring. You know that belongs to him, right? Only his mate can wear it."

I glance at the ring. I can feel his magic. He is not a witch, but each paranormal creature has their own signature.

"I don't know," I say, and then another jolt reminds me of my mission. "I don't have the time to deal with it anyway. My job has to be done. That stone needs to be retrieved."

"What did the call say?"

"It only mentioned lightning, and it said that only a god can have the stone. I need to search for it in the land of the north, the home of those who worship him."

Celestia is good at helping me figure out where I need to start when the relics don't give me all the details. "I know where you need to go to find this place," she says. "But I'll need a book to show you."

∼

THE LADY

"Selena?" I scream at my assistant from my office door.

When she enters my room, she seems breathless." Yes, my lady?"

I clench my fists, trying to keep my composure. "We lost not only the Stone of Destiny, but the ring I gave them to open the magic gate."

Selena lowers her eyes. "Yes, my Lady, that's what Donovan reports. He also said that the witch Lilandra has been killed during the mission, but her mentee, Juniper, escaped with a man, a shifter."

But I already read the report. They arrived yesterday night. That shifter will only be trouble for us. I'm thrilled that Lilandra is off of our back, yet it seems that her mentee may be worse than her.

I turn to my assistant. "What do you have on him? We need to know their weaknesses, so we can defeat them."

Selena shakes her head and studies a sheet of paper she holds in her hand. "The only things that we know about him make no sense. First, he can kill demons with his bare hands and the other piece of information I have is that he has wings. I don't know what to think of this, my Lady."

I take Selena's paper and study the image on it. "Impossible."

It's not happening. It can't be. I'm old enough to know that tail.

Selena moves closer. "What is it, my Lady?"

"You said he could kill demons and that he has wings?"

"Yes, my Lady, that was the last transmission that we received from the second crew just before they were crushed to death inside the tunnel." She looks at me and then the paper now in my hand. "Is something wrong?"

"What did Donovan have to say about that?"

"He didn't see anything since they took a different tunnel. We discovered multiple ways to enter the place."

I give the paper back to Selena and start pacing.

She remains standing and waits for my next move. Finally, she asks, "Do we need to search for something about him?"

I shake my head. "No, I know what he is. It's just that they were supposed to be fairy tales. They disappeared so many centuries ago."

"What, my Lady?"

"He is simply a dragon shifter."

Selena's expression turns perplexed. "Dragon shifter?"

"Yes. I thought they were only a children's story. Could

this mean he's found his mate? Could it be her? Could she be his mate?"

"What do you mean, my Lady?" She frowns. "You mean that Juniper girl?"

"Yes, if that is the case that only seems to be trouble for us. Dragon Shifters are the strongest creatures. Not do they have shifter powers, but also magic of their own. All because of Merlin's story, the pact he made with them."

"I don't understand."

"Tell Donovan that he needs to go where the north people once lived. I will provide more details very soon. The only way that we can increase our power is with the fear of the god."

CHAPTER TWENTY-ONE

DRAKE

MY BODY CLENCHES AS THE ORGASM ROCKS THROUGH ME.

I'm in my bed, in the room next door to Juniper's, not fully awake, but not fully asleep either.

Yeah, that definitely tells me she started the mating dreams. It was cut short by something, but I don't know what.

I awaken and clean up, then I leave the bedroom and hit the corridor. I know she's supposed to be right beside me, the way the Elder told me. My beast tells me she's not in her room anymore.

"Sorry. You just missed her."

I turn around. "Oh, it's you, little one."

She raises her hand. "I know. I already asked her what she was going to do about her mate."

I look at her. "What did she say?"

Celestia shifts from foot to foot, clearly uncomfortable.

"You can tell me. I won't be mad at you."

She sighs. "Well, she said that she didn't have time for a mate. She is here for her job and her job only."

I could see that Juniper's answer made Celestia sad. But I laugh, and the sound echoes in the corridor. "Yeah, that's what I thought. She left, right?"

Celestia nods at me. "She got a call again."

"What? Already?"

She sighs. "I know. I told her those magic objects need to learn about vacation time. She said that neither the relics nor the people chasing them know anything about time off."

I smile. Juniper is full of sass. This will be a fun chase, and it will be amazing when I catch her. But, at the same time, I'm worried. I can't leave her alone, since she might get herself killed.

"Any ideas where she's off to?"

Celestia smiles mischievously. "I do. I helped her figure it out. You see, in a lot of those calls she receives, there's only vague information about what is calling her or where it is located. So, I provide my assistance where I can."

She left us, well that only means the chase is on. "So, where is she going?"

"Denmark."

"She went to see the Vikings?"

Celestia starts to laugh. "How long has it been since when you were awake? Vikings are ancient history now, but the people of Denmark are their descendants for sure. The only clue Juniper got from the relic was lightning, and it told her the people of the north worshipped a god of thunder in the past and that only that god can have it."

I nod. "That can only mean Thor Odin son, as per the legend. He created the thunder and lightning."

"Exactly. Ever met them?"

"No, I never did. I am old enough to have met them, but

I don't like the cold there. During that period I was closer to England. What is it?"

She's looking at me like I'm a weird creature. "How old are you?"

I smile. "I am old enough. I stopped counting so many centuries ago and then I slept more than a few centuries ... I've forgotten how old it makes me." I pause. I can tell she wants to ask a question. "What is it?"

"Do you remember your parents?"

I don't answer. Yes, I do a little, but my memories are vague about that period of my life. That's one part I'm not ready to explore. "That belongs to me and my mate. She needs to be the first to know."

She nods. "So, you're up for a chase?"

I smirk. "Of course. Not only did I kiss her, but she has my ring, and she's starting to have mating dreams. If I don't join her, those dreams will get worse. I have to be there the moment she's ready to join with me."

She puts up both of her hands. "Wha! I may have died a century ago, but my ears are still chaste, so please don't start explaining that mating dream of yours now. I knew something like that was happening before she received the call, though, since I saw your magic energy all over her when she woke up."

I open my mouth to speak.

She shakes her head. "I don't know if now is the time to understand all this anyway. You've got to go after her and be with her. You know what she does. It's dangerous."

I could ask questions for hours. "You're right. Thanks for the tips."

Celestia follows me outside. It's not possible to shift inside those underground tunnels. There's not enough space. "You're going to shift here?"

I don't want to explain — part of my magic makes

humans see nothing. Maybe a few will see it, but who will believe them?

I remove my clothes quickly, and Celestia turns around. No shifters are prudish. None. I shift, flap my wings and begin to fly. My beast is looking for Juniper's energy. Sure, her teleporting might make it more difficult to trace her, but it's not impossible. Since I know which direction I need to take to fly after her, it will be easy to find her magic energy through my beast's eyes.

I gain altitude. My mate needs me. Maybe she doesn't want me yet, but she still needs me to keep her alive. After that, we will see what time will bring. It will be interesting to see where life will lead us and what her missions will be.

I let my beast take control, and I let him fly us in the direction of Denmark. I hope Juniper's call will be worth it.

THE END

ALSO BY NADINE TRAVERS

Urban Fantasy

Supertunatural Intelligence Agency

Vampire on the run

Blood Rebellion

A Lilandra Reeves Adventure

Seal of Solomon

Juniper Samoni Trilogy

The Stone of Destiny - January 11th 2021

Menage Series

A MFM Boss Romance Series

Billionaires Assistant

Billionaires Assistant On The Run (Coming Soon)

Romantic Suspense

The Mercenaries Series

Renegade

Hacker - February 2021

Sensei (Coming Soon)

ABOUT THE AUTHOR

Dear readers, I hope you love the story. You can follow me
here.

Website: http://www.nadinetravers.com
Series website: https://www.
supernaturalintelligenceagency.com
Facebook: https://www.
facebook.com/NadineTraversWriter/
Twitter: https://twitter.com/NadineWriter
Goodreads: https://www.
goodreads.com/nadinetravers

Enjoyed this book? You can make a big difference

Reviews are the most powerful tool in my arsenal when it
comes to getting attention for my books. Much as I'd like to,
I don't have the financial muscle of a New York publisher. I
can't take-out full-page ads in the newspaper or put posters
on the subway.
(Not yet, anyway)
But I do have something much more powerful and effective
than that, and it's something that those publishers would kill
to get their hands on.
A committed and loyal bunch of readers.
Honest reviews of my books help bring them to the attention
of other readers.

If you've enjoyed this book, I would be very grateful if you could spend just five minutes leaving
a review (it can be as short as you like) of the books on any platform you download it.
Thank you very much.

Newsletter: https://landing.mailerlite.com/webforms/ landing/e5hou3

Nadine

facebook.com/NadineTraversWriter
twitter.com/NadineWriter

Made in the USA
Middletown, DE
03 December 2020